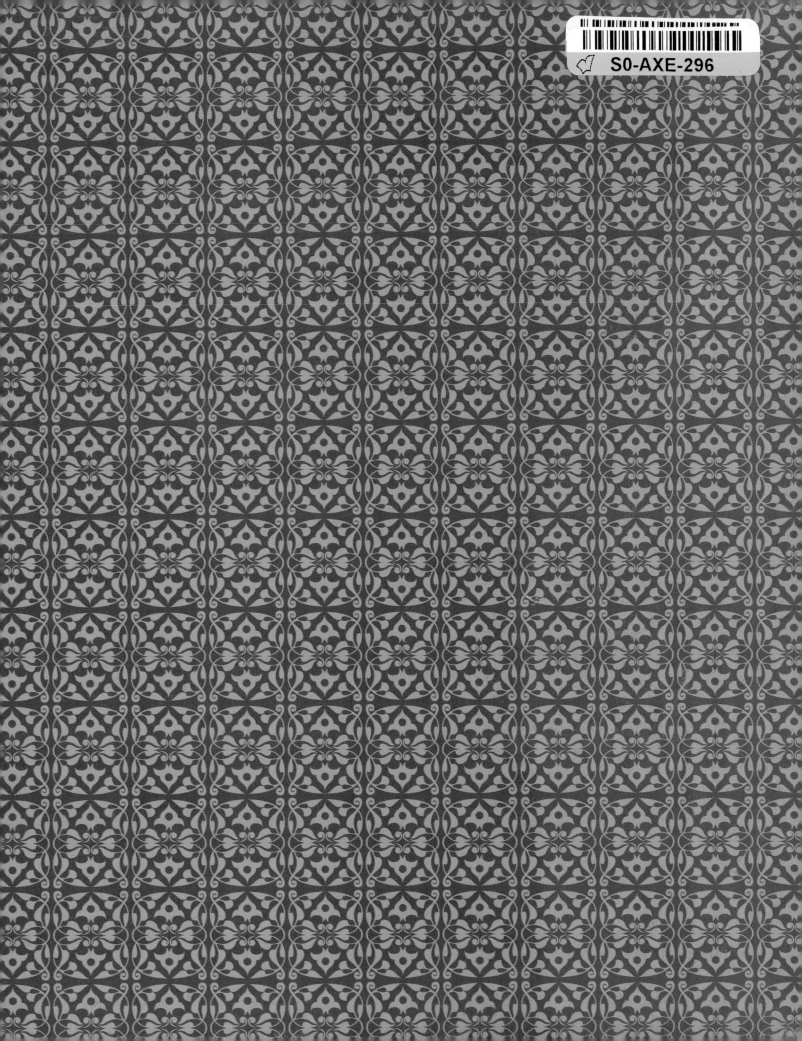

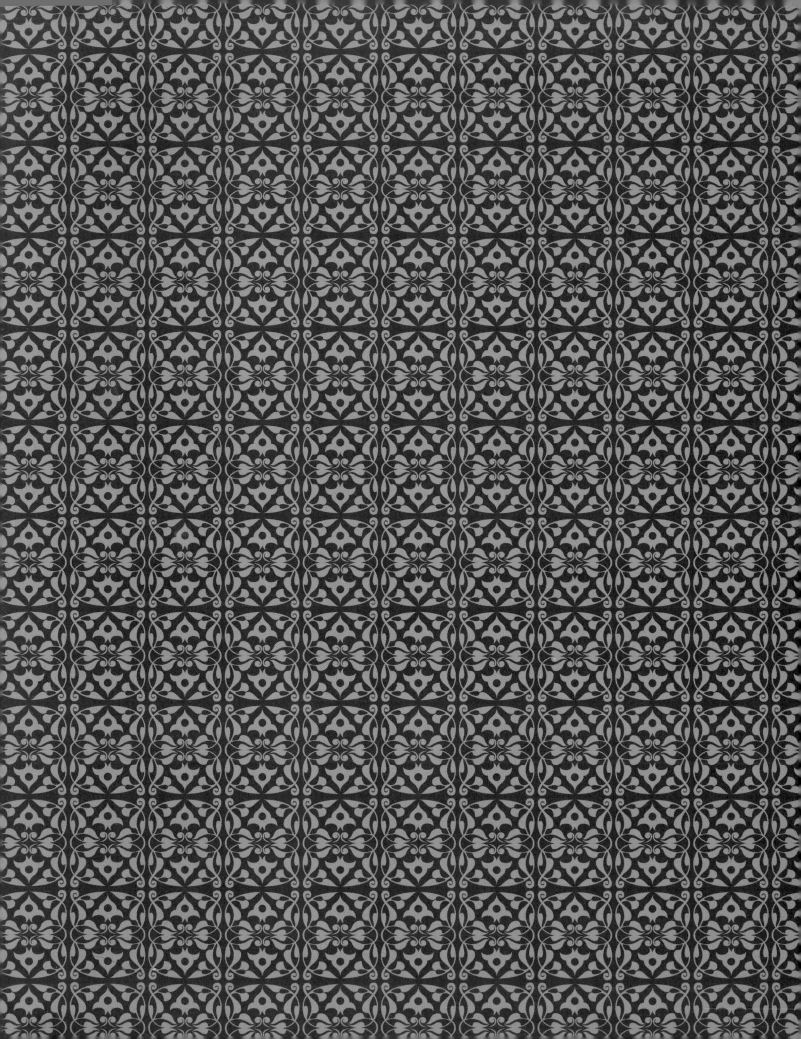

CLASSIC
CHILDREN'S
STORIES

PUBLICATIONS INTERNATIONAL, LTD.

Cover illustrated by Krista Brauckmann-Towns
Title page illustrated by Holly Jones

Louis Weber, C.E.O.
Publications International, Ltd.
7373 North Cicero Avenue
Lincolnwood, Illinois 60646

ISBN: 0-7853-3458-0

Once upon a time...

CONTENTS

The Ant and the Grasshopper

Adapted by Catherine McCafferty
Illustrated by Jason Wolff

Summer had just begun. Animals and insects scurried about, enjoying the summer sun. "Summer's here! The best time of the year!" the Grasshopper sang. His joyful jumps took him from the cool shade of a bush into bright rays of the sun. "Warm sun, lots of fun!" he added to his song.

A line of ants marched past the Grasshopper, carrying small seeds and bits of food. As they walked along, some crumbs fell to the ground. Before the ants could get them, the Grasshopper had eaten the crumbs.

The biggest ant, at the end of the line, walked up to the Grasshopper. "We've worked very hard to gather this food," said the Ant. "You should have helped us pick up what we dropped."

"That's what's wrong with your summer song," the Grasshopper sang. Then he said, "You're always working. Summertime is for play, not work."

"Summertime is for planning and gathering," said the Ant. "It's time for getting all the food we will need for the winter."

"Winter is so far away, I think I'd rather go and play," said the Grasshopper. He was about to hop away when the Ant stopped him.

"Wait! What about the food you took from us?" the Ant asked.

"Oh, yes. Thank you." The Grasshopper pointed toward a field. "And over there is a whole field of wheat to replace your crumbs. I like cornfields better myself, but that might be too far for you to walk." And the Grasshopper hopped off to the cornfield.

The Grasshopper leaped onto a cornstalk. A soft leaf gave him a bed. Above him, another leaf gave him shade. And within reach, smaller, tender leaves gave him food. There was even an ear of fresh corn nearby.

"Those ants can gather and work and store. I'll just snooze right here and snore." He fell fast asleep.

Meanwhile, the Ant lined the tunnels of his home with seeds and other foods. "When the snow is on the ground, we will be nice and warm in our nest. We will have plenty of food to eat and plenty of time to play," thought the Ant.

All that summer, the Grasshopper watched the ants. When he saw them going to a picnic for crumbs, he hopped along to eat his fill. While they carried food back to their nest, he slept in his cornstalk bed.

Then one day, the Grasshopper heard a loud noise. The farmer was coming to harvest the corn! The Grasshopper jumped off his leafy bed and ran into the grass. Down came the leaves and the corn the Grasshopper had feasted on all summer. Down came the leaves that had sheltered him.

"Close call, all in all," sang the Grasshopper. "Did you see that?" he asked the Ant as the line of ants marched past. "I just lost my bed and food!"

The Ant stopped. "The days are getting shorter, my friend. But there is still time for you to store food and find a winter shelter."

The Grasshopper thought about that for a second. "Not today, I've got to play," he sang and hopped his way through the grass. When he found a toadstool, he said, "This will put a roof over my head. So I'll just eat later . . . instead," he added, to make a rhyme.

The Grasshopper had just fallen asleep when he heard a plop! The next thing he knew, his toadstool was falling over.

"Oh, I'm sorry," chattered a squirrel above him. "My paws were so full of nuts that I dropped some. You can have them if you like."

The Grasshopper hopped away. "I don't like nuts, no if's, and's, or but's."

All throughout the fields and forests, he saw squirrels gathering nuts. They chattered to one another, "I found more!" "Have you heard? This winter is going to be very snowy!" and "I think I have enough, but I want to be sure. It's going to be a long winter!" All this work was making it very hard to play, and to sleep. In a corner of the hay field, the Grasshopper found a small, sunny rock. He was just settling down, when the ants began marching by him again.

"You again!" he said to the Ant. "I thought by now you'd have enough. You can't eat all that stuff!"

The Ant smiled, but he did not stop to talk. "It's always better to have a little extra than not enough," he called over his shoulder.

The Grasshopper frowned. The sun had moved, and the rock was cold. At the other end of the field, the farmer was cutting hay. "Doesn't anybody here know when to play?" he asked.

He hopped off to the apple orchard. Most of the leaves were gone from the tree. But the Grasshopper found a few small apples on the ground. He munched on them until he was full. Then he settled in for a nap near the root of the tree. The Grasshopper shivered. He looked around for a sunny spot, but the sun was already gone from the sky. "Someone needs to tell the sun that its working day is not done," he sang unhappily.

The sun was one thing the Grasshopper didn't mind seeing at work. With each day, though, it seemed to work less and less.

The ground seemed colder, too. One day, when the Grasshopper tried to nibble an apple, he found that it was frozen. "I don't like my apple in ice," said the Grasshopper. He was so chilly that it was hard to think of a second line to his rhyme. "Ice, nice, rice, mice. . . ."

The Grasshopper tried to think of something nice. "A warm place with lots of rice," he sang in a shivery voice. He didn't especially like rice, but he was getting hungry. Then he thought, "Maybe I'll visit my friends, the mice." The Grasshopper crept into the home of the field mouse family. It was warm inside. There was no sign of rice, but the Grasshopper was sure they would have something else nice.

"Thank you for visiting, Mr. Grasshopper," said Mother Mouse. "I would invite you to stay, but all of my sisters and brothers are moving in for the winter. Isn't that nice? Oh, here they are now!"

A crowd of mice rushed into the nest. It was nice to see them hugging each other. But the Grasshopper wanted the kind of nice that meant he had a place to live and something to eat. The Grasshopper hopped back to the orchard. The ground was so cold that it hurt his tiny feet.

"Where are those ants, now that I need them?" sang the Grasshopper.

The Grasshopper found his apple on the ground, but it was still frozen. The Grasshopper thought and thought. Finally he said, "Maybe I'll take this apple to feed the ants." He pushed. And he tugged. And he kicked. But after an hour, he had moved the heavy, icy apple just one foot farther in the cold snow.

"How do those ants carry such heavy things over such long distances?" he wondered. "They're even smaller than me." As the Grasshopper stood there thinking, snow began to fall on the ground. The snowflakes slowly covered the Grasshopper. With a jump, he fluttered his wings.

He had to get inside or he would freeze just like the apple! Hopping as fast as he could, the Grasshopper raced to the Ant's home. He hopped between the snowflakes and over snowbanks. Soon the Grasshopper was standing outside the opening to the Ant's house. "Anybody home?" he called as he stepped into the tunnels.

"Hello, Grasshopper," said the wise Ant. "Why aren't you singing and playing out in the snow?"

The Grasshopper wanted to say that he had just come by for a visit and would leave shortly, but he could feel the cold wind on his back. Sadly, the Grasshopper sang, "I should have listened to what you said. Now I'm cold and scared and unfed." It wasn't his best song, but he hoped the Ant would understand.

Luckily, the Ant did understand. But he wanted to make sure that the Grasshopper understood, too. So he said, "We got our food for the winter by working hard, Grasshopper. If you stay with us this winter, you'll have to work hard, too."

The Grasshopper gulped. What if it was a long winter, like the squirrels said? But then he remembered the icy apple in the snow. Proudly, he sang, "I tried to work once this year. I tried to roll an apple here."

The Ant nodded. "Perhaps there is some hope for you, Grasshopper," he said. "Your job here will be to sing for us. Every day." Then the Ant laughed, "Because winter is our time to play."

The Grasshopper agreed to the Ant's offer, and he started right away. Quickly, he hopped onto an old spool of thread in the middle of the room. He sang and danced for the ants, while they slept and baked and played.

"Winter can be icy cold, so I'll do as I've been told. I'll sing and kick for these kind ants in this warm wintertime dance," the Grasshopper sang as he kicked his feet and waved his hat into the air. Some of the ants danced about the room to the Grasshopper's wintertime song.

All that winter, the Grasshopper sang for the Ant and his family. And the very next summer, the Grasshopper sang a new song as he helped gather food. "Summer work is slow and steady. But when winter comes, I'll be ready!"

Gulliver's Travels

Adapted by Brian Conway
Illustrated by Karen Stormer Brooks

Gulliver was a doctor in the city of London. He grew tired of the crowded city, though, and decided to take a trip on a ship. He wanted to journey to distant lands and see many different people and things. He had no idea his voyage would take him to strange places that can't be found on any maps. This is the story of the little land of Lilliput, the first stop in Gulliver's many travels.

Sailing through the East Indies, the ship hit a terrible storm. Gulliver and five other sailors had to leave the sinking ship behind. They climbed into a small boat and dropped it into the stormy sea. At the mercy of the violent waves, the boat twisted and turned until suddenly it flipped over. The men tried to swim against the waves, but the water swallowed up Gulliver and his shipmates.

Gulliver awoke on a grassy shore. He could not move, but he thought he felt something moving steadily up his leg to his chest. He shifted his blurry eyes to see what seemed to be a tiny human being who was not much bigger than a spoon.

When he felt many more of these little people marching up his leg, Gulliver tried to lift his head. His hair, he found, was tied down, and his arms and legs were tied down, too. He struggled to lift one arm, breaking the tiny strings that bound it to the ground. Then he broke the strings near his head, making it easier for him to examine his surroundings.

He saw hundreds of the tiny creatures staring back at him. Some ran away from this massive human, while others shot arrows the size of needles at his free hand. Gulliver stayed still until he heard one little man talking to him in a language he could not understand.

Gulliver politely agreed with everything the little man said. This man must be their emperor, Gulliver thought. The emperor spoke kindly for the most part, and Gulliver did nothing to upset the small creatures. He did lift his hand again, however, to point to his mouth.

The emperor understood that he was hungry. He ordered basket upon basket of breads and meats to be carried up to Gulliver's mouth and dropped in.

Then the emperor pointed off into the distance and called for a cart that 500 tiny carpenters had built. The small creatures untied him. Gulliver cooperatively climbed onto the cart and allowed them to chain him to it. Then 900 of their strongest men pulled him to their capital city.

They tugged Gulliver to their largest building, an ancient temple just outside the magnificent little city. There they bound him in chains at the ankles. Gulliver understood their fear and their need to protect themselves from being trampled. He did not mind the chains too much, and he felt honored to stay in their temple. He could crawl in and lay down with only his feet sticking out.

Now Gulliver was eager, as always, to learn about this place and its tiny people. He crouched down to the ground and made every effort to speak with them. The emperor sent the finest scholars in the land to visit with Gulliver every day for several weeks. Soon, Gulliver learned that the curious kingdom was called Lilliput, and its gentle, intelligent people were known as Lilliputians.

The first words Gulliver learned to say to the Lilliputians were, "Please remove my chains." They told him it would take some time to remove them, and Gulliver understood well. They fed him regularly, after all, and he had no complaints.

Before too long the Lilliputians were no longer afraid of Gulliver. They fondly called him "The Man-Mountain" and came to see him often. They let Gulliver pick them up in his hand. That way, he could talk to them without crouching.

He showed them his coins and his pen, which they studied with great curiosity. The Lilliputians were especially amazed with Gulliver's pocket watch. Its ticking was very noisy to them, but they had many questions about how it worked.

Even the children of Lilliput came to love Gulliver. They would dance on his hand and play hide-and-seek in his hair. Gulliver enjoyed amusing the children. He wondered what he could do to entertain the other Lilliputians.

One day the army of Lilliput marched out to a field to practice its drills. The Lilliputians were very proud of their army, and Gulliver himself was fascinated with the soldiers' skill. Gulliver built a stage for their exercises. He used his handkerchief and several sticks to build the playing field.

He picked up 24 horses and 24 soldiers and put them on the stage. Then he lifted the emperor and his court in his hand so they could see the maneuvers from above. They liked this very much. So much, in fact, the emperor ordered that this entertainment be performed daily for everyone.

Then the day came when Gulliver would be released from his chains. But first Gulliver had to pledge an oath to the emperor. He stood before the emperor in the position that the law required, then he gladly made the promises they asked him to make.

"The Man-Mountain" promised to be forever careful where he walked. He agreed to deliver the emperor's important messages over great distances in little time. And he offered to help the Lilliputian army in times of war.

In return, the Lilliputians gave Gulliver his freedom and agreed to give him as much food as he could eat.

A few weeks later, the emperor visited Gulliver. He told Gulliver that the Lilliputians were getting ready for a battle. For many hundreds of years, the emperor explained, the Lilliputians had been at war with the only other kingdom they knew, an island nation called Blefuscu.

Long ago, Gulliver was told, the emperor of Lilliput and the emperor of Blefuscu had an argument over which end of an egg is best to crack first.

"It is only logical to break the egg on the larger end!" shouted the emperor of Blefuscu.

"Only idiots would break the egg on the larger end! It is only logical to break the egg on the smaller end, of course!" the emperor of Lilliput shouted back.

That argument became a war that had never ended, and Blefuscu was now sending a large fleet of ships to attack Lilliput. The emperor asked for Gulliver's help.

Gulliver's job was to stop Blefuscu's ships before they reached the shores of Lilliput. He asked for several strong cables and a set of iron bars. Gulliver bent the bars into hooks and tied them to the cables.

The sea between the two kingdoms was much too deep for tiny humans, but Gulliver could walk easily through the water in very little time. He set out on his own across the sea.

Gulliver soon met the enemy ships as they left the shores of Blefuscu. He rose from the water and frightened the Blefuscudians terribly. Most of them dove from their ships at the sight of him and swam back to shore.

Some brave Blefuscudians stayed on their ships to shoot arrows at their giant foe. When Gulliver attached the hooks to their ships and started to pull them away, though, even the most fearless soldiers leaped from their ships to the water below.

Gulliver tugged the ships back to Lilliput. Great cheers rose from the shore as he came closer, holding the entire fleet of Blefuscu in one of his massive hands.

"Long live the emperor of Lilliput!" cried Gulliver.

The emperor greeted Gulliver with great excitement. "You shall be granted the highest title of honor," the emperor said to Gulliver.

Then the emperor asked Gulliver to bring the rest of Blefuscu's ships into Lilliput's port, so that he could conquer the island of Blefuscu and become its emperor, too. But Gulliver quickly refused, and this made the emperor of Lilliput very angry.

When the people of Blefuscu heard this news, they sent an ambassador to greet Gulliver with an offer of peace. Gulliver agreed to visit the island of Blefuscu very soon.

But first Gulliver had to receive permission from the emperor of Lilliput to leave his island. "I wish to bring peace to both countries," Gulliver told the emperor of Lilliput.

"There will never be peace between our countries until they agree that the smaller end of an egg must be broken first," said the emperor of Lilliput. "But I cannot stop you from leaving. I wish you well, my friend." With the emperor's reluctant permission, Gulliver prepared to visit the island of Blefuscu.

After many hours of wondering how he would travel to Blefuscu, Gulliver decided that the best way would be simply to walk there. He put on his hat and began wading through the water. Soon, Gulliver arrived at the shores of Blefuscu.

The people of Blefuscu were very happy to see "The Man-Mountain." They greeted him with flowers and a large feast. Gulliver was happy to see them, too. He did not want them to be afraid of him, and he knew he had much to learn about their customs.

Gulliver spent two fine days on the island of Blefuscu. Many teachers came together to teach the giant man. Gulliver held them in his hand as they talked about their laws and customs. On the third day, while he took a walk on the beach, Gulliver spotted an empty boat in the sea. It was a real boat for a man just his size!

Gulliver hurried to thank the Blefuscudians for their kindness, then he rowed the boat back to Lilliput to bid his dear friends a fond farewell. The emperor presented him with several live cows and plenty of food for his journey. Then Gulliver sailed away.

Before long, Gulliver spotted the sail of a ship like the one he had once sailed on. He rowed swiftly to it and was welcomed aboard. He told the crew about his voyage to Lilliput. No one believed his story until he reached into his pocket and pulled out the tiny cattle he had received from the emperor. That was more than enough to convince them.

Soon Gulliver was back in London, where people came to see his tiny animals. Gulliver told them stories about his journey, and he prepared for his next incredible voyage to faraway lands.

Hiawatha

Written by Henry Wadsworth Longfellow
Illustrated by Holly Jones

By the shores of Gitche Gumee,

By the shining Big-Sea-Water,

Stood the wigwam of Nokomis,

Daughter of the Moon, Nokomis.

Dark behind it rose the forest,

Rose the black and gloomy pine-trees,

Rose the firs with cones upon them;

Bright before it beat the water

Beat the clear and sunny water

Beat the shining Big-Sea-Water.

There the wrinkled, old Nokomis

Nursed the little Hiawatha,

Rocked him in his linden cradle,

Bedded soft in moss and rushes,

Safely bound with reindeer sinews;

Stilled his fretful wail by saying,

"Hush! the Naked Bear will get thee!"

Lulled him into slumber, singing,

"Ewa-yea! my little owlet!

Who is this, that lights the wigwam?

With his great eyes lights the wigwam?

Ewa-yea! my little owlet!"

Many things Nokomis taught him

Of the stars that shine in heaven;

Showed him Ishkoodah, the comet,

Ishkoodah, with fiery tresses;

Showed the Death-Dance of the spirits,

Warriors with their plumes and war-clubs,

Flaring far away to Northward

In the frosty nights of Winter;

Showed the broad, white road in heaven,

Pathway of the ghosts, the shadows.

Running straight across the heavens,

Crowded with the ghosts, the shadows.

At the door on Summer evenings

Sat the little Hiawatha;

Heard the whispering of the pine-trees,

Heard the lapping of the water,

Sounds of music, words of wonder.

Saw the fire-fly, Wah-wah-taysee,

Flitting through the dusk of evening,

With the twinkle of its candle

Lighting up the brakes and bushes,

And he sang the song of children,

Sang the song Nokomis taught him:

"Wah-wah-taysee, little fire-fly,

Little, flitting, white-fire insect.

Little, dancing, white-fire creature,

Light me with your little candle,

Ere upon my bed I lay me,

Ere in sleep I close my eyelids!"

Saw the moon rise from the water

Rippling, rounding from the water,

Saw the flecks and shadows on it,

Whispered, "What is that, Nokomis?"

And the good Nokomis answered:

"Once a warrior, very angry,

Seized his grandmother, and threw her

Up into the sky at midnight;

Right against the moon he threw her;

'T is her body that you see there."

Saw the rainbow in the heaven,

In the eastern sky, the rainbow,

Whispered, "What is that, Nokomis?"

And the good Nokomis answered:

"'T is the heaven of flowers you see there;

All the wild-flowers of the forest,

All the lilies of the prairie,

When on earth they fade and perish,

Blossom in that heaven above us."

When he heard the owls at midnight,

Hooting, laughing in the forest,

"What is that?" he cried in terror:

"What is that," he said, "Nokomis?"

And the good Nokomis answered:

"That is but the owl and owlet,

Talking in their native language,

Talking, scolding at each other."

Then the little Hiawatha,

Learned of every bird its language,

Learned their names and all their secrets,

How they built their nests in Summer

Where they hid themselves in Winter,

Talked with them whene'er he met them,

Called them "Hiawatha's Chickens."

Of all beasts he learned the language,

Learned their names and all their secrets,

How the beavers built their lodges,

Where the squirrels hid their acorns,

How the reindeer ran so swiftly,

Why the rabbit was so timid,

Talked with them whene'er he met them,

Called them "Hiawatha's Brothers."

Thumbelina

Adapted by Megan Musgrave
Illustrated by Jane Maday

There was once a woman who lived in a tiny cottage which had the most beautiful garden in the world. She was very happy tending her garden, but over time she became sad. She had no children who could share her garden with her. She decided to visit the old witch in her village and ask for her help.

When the woman explained that she wanted a child, the old witch thought for a moment. Then she pulled a tiny bag out of a fold in her cloak. "Plant these wildflower seeds and tend them carefully every day. Soon you will have your wish," said the old witch.

The woman took the seeds home with her. The next day, she planted them in a sunny corner of her garden. She watered them and watched over them every day.

Soon tiny green sprouts began to poke up out of the ground. Before long, the sprouts grew and blossomed into a beautiful patch of wildflowers.

In the center of the wildflower patch grew a single, beautiful tulip. Its deep pink petals were closed up tightly. The flower was so lovely that the woman could not resist bending down to smell it. As she knelt in front of the flower, its petals suddenly opened. The woman was amazed to find a tiny girl sitting inside the open tulip. She wore a tulip petal for a dress and had long, gleaming hair.

"You are the most beautiful child I have ever seen! And you are hardly even as big as my thumb. Would you like to stay with me in my garden?" asked the woman.

"Oh, yes!" replied the tiny girl.

"I will call you Thumbelina," said the woman. She made Thumbelina a tiny bed out of a shiny acorn shell. The tiny girl slept soundly, kept warm by her rose petal blanket.

Thumbelina and her mother lived very happily in the garden the whole summer long. Thumbelina loved to play in the little pond in the middle of the garden, so her mother made her a tiny boat out of a maple leaf. Thumbelina rowed around the pond, using two blades of grass as oars. Her mother sat by the side of the pond and read stories to her while she played.

Sometimes, Thumbelina sang as she rowed. She had a beautiful, silvery voice that her mother always loved to hear.

One day, a frog was hopping by the garden. He heard Thumbelina's beautiful voice and came near the pond. When he saw the tiny girl rowing her maple leaf boat he said, "I've never seen such a beautiful creature! I must take her away to my lily pad to be my wife."

The frog watched and waited until Thumbelina's mother went inside the cottage to get a cup of lemonade for Thumbelina. Then the frog jumped out from behind the reeds where he had been hiding and captured Thumbelina. He carried her away to the river where he lived and placed her on a lily pad. "Rest here while I go and make the plans for our wedding," said the frog. With that, he hopped away.

Thumbelina did not want to be the wife of a frog. She wanted to be at home with her mother again. She became so sad that she began to cry. Her tiny tears fell into the river and made ripples in its glassy surface.

When the fish in the river saw Thumbelina crying, they decided to help her. They nibbled through the stem of her lily pad until it broke free and floated down the river, far away from the frog.

Thumbelina flowed gently on the river until finally the lily pad came to rest on a green, grassy bank of the river.

Thumbelina climbed up the bank and found herself on the edge of a grassy meadow. "This will be a fine place for me to live until I can find my way back to Mother again," she said.

She wove herself a tiny hammock out of grass blades and hung it up beneath a large daisy which sheltered her from the dew at night. During the day she wandered through the meadow. If she was thirsty, she drank the dew off a blade of grass. If she was hungry, she had a bite of clover or some honeysuckle. She became friends with the butterflies and ladybugs in the meadow, and at night she slept safely under her daisy roof.

One day, Thumbelina noticed that the days were getting chilly. The flowers of the meadow were fading, and the leaves were turning bright shades of orange, red, and yellow and dropping from the trees. Fall was coming. Soon so many leaves were falling that it was all Thumbelina could do to keep out from under them.

The nights were becoming colder, too. She made herself a blanket out of cotton from the meadow, but soon it was not enough to keep her warm at night. "How will I keep warm in the winter?" cried Thumbelina. She began to take long walks, looking for a place where she could be safe and warm for the winter. One day, she found a small burrow inside a tree. She poked her head inside to see if anyone lived there.

Inside the little burrow lived a friendly old field mouse. The burrow was snug and cozy, for the mouse had lined it with cotton and hay from the meadow. "Excuse me," said Thumbelina quietly, "may I come into your warm burrow for a moment?"

The old field mouse almost never had any visitors in autumn, and she was very happy to have one now. "Come in, come in! You poor dear, you'll catch your death of cold. Come over by the fire and have a cup of tea."

Thumbelina and the field mouse were soon fast friends. The field mouse invited Thumbelina to stay with her for the winter. Together they gathered nuts, grains, and berries for the cold months ahead. Thumbelina sang songs and told her friend stories of her adventures, while the field mouse cooked their dinner or sewed by the fire.

One day it began to snow outside. Thumbelina had never seen snow before, so she opened the door of the burrow to peek outside. Some of the snowflakes were almost as big as she was! She loved to watch them dance in the air and come to rest gently on the ground. But as she watched the snow fall she saw something strange. Lying near the field mouse's front door was a young sparrow with a broken wing. He was shivering as the snow began to cover him.

Thumbelina called to the field mouse. Together they helped the sparrow into the burrow. They warmed the sparrow by the fire until the snowflakes melted off his feathers. After they fed him some soup, he was able to speak.

"I injured myself as my friends and I were flying south for the winter," chirped the sparrow. "I would have frozen to death if you hadn't found me and warmed me by the fire. Thank you for being so kind and taking me into your home."

"You are welcome," said the kind field mouse. "You may stay here as long as you like."

Thumbelina, the sparrow, and the field mouse passed a wonderful winter together in the warm burrow. The field mouse prepared tasty meals for her new friends, and Thumbelina helped mend the sparrow's wing so that he would be able to fly again when spring came.

Thumbelina told stories about her mother and the wonderful garden where she was born. She danced and entertained her friends until they laughed with delight. When the sparrow was strong enough, he told tales about flying high above the trees.

One day, Thumbelina poked her head outside the burrow again. The snow was nearly melted, and tiny green shoots were beginning to appear all over the meadow. "Spring is coming!" she shouted to her friends.

Thumbelina, the sparrow, and the field mouse jumped for joy. Winter was finally over! They cleaned the burrow from top to bottom and prepared for spring to come.

Soon the days were warm and sunny again. Flowers grew from the green grass. The sparrow decided it was time to leave the burrow. "Thumbelina," he said, "you saved my life. Now I would like to help you find your mother." Thumbelina knew she would miss the field mouse and the warm burrow very much, but she longed to see her mother again. Thumbelina said good-bye to her field mouse friend and climbed onto the sparrow's back.

Thumbelina held on tight to the sparrow's feathers as he flew high above the trees and away from the meadow. Thumbelina sang songs about flying as they flew over fields and ponds. At night, as the two friends slept, they covered themselves with leaves to stay warm.

After many days, the sparrow soared over the river where Thumbelina had traveled on her lily pad. "This looks familiar!" Thumbelina shouted.

"We're getting very close to your home," the sparrow said.

Thumbelina was very excited. She thought about her home and the garden. "Do you think we will ever find my mother again?" Thumbelina asked her friend.

"Yes, but first I have something special to show you," said the sparrow. He flew deep into the forest and landed gently in a thicket. Sunlight streamed into the thicket from between the great trees above. All around them, beautiful flowers of every color blossomed.

"This must be a magical place," said Thumbelina.

And indeed it was.

No sooner had Thumbelina said this, than a beautiful lily opened before her. Out stepped a tiny boy, no bigger than a thumb. He wore a crown on his head, and he had a beautiful pair of shiny wings.

"I am the Prince of the Flowers," said the boy. "You are the kindest girl I have ever known. Come and live with us here and be the Princess of the Flowers." With that, the meadow came alive. Tiny people stepped out of the flowers all around Thumbelina. She had never been so happy! They gave her a pair of beautiful, silvery wings, and she lived with them in the magical thicket, where it was summer all the time and never grew cold.

The Prince knew that Thumbelina missed her mother. One day he flew with Thumbelina to the cottage where her mother still lived. The woman was so overjoyed to see her tiny daughter. From that day on, Thumbelina and the Prince played in the garden and told her mother stories of their magical life in the forest.

The Cat That Walked by Himself

Adapted by Lisa Harkrader
Illustrated by Jon Goodell

Long ago, when the world was quite wild, all the animals and the men and women were wild as well. They lived their wild lives in the forest.

One day Dog, Horse, Cow, and Cat gathered on a hill. They watched as Man and Woman built a stone house in the valley below. They saw Man and Woman gather soft leaves and pine needles and carry them into the stone house for a bed. They saw Man and Woman stretch a hide over the entrance of the stone house for a door.

"Man and Woman won't be wild for much longer," said Cat. "I would never give up my freedom to live in a stone house. I am a Cat, and I walk by myself."

Dog, Horse, Cow, and Cat watched Man carry twigs and logs inside. Soon the house glowed with the light of a fire.

"They'll be warm tonight," said Dog. "Warmer than we'll be out here in the forest."

The animals watched Woman moving about inside the house, poking at the fire with a stick.

Dog lifted his nose in the air and sniffed. "Roast mutton," he said. "Maybe I'll go down to see if they're happy in their house. Does anyone want to come along?"

"It isn't wise to venture so near to humans," said Horse.

"The very idea makes me shudder in fear," said Cow.

"No, thank you," said Cat. "I am a Cat, and I walk by myself." He leaped into a tree and pretended to curl up for a nap.

Dog raced down the hill. Cat followed quietly through the woods behind him.

Cat watched the Woman give Dog a mutton bone. Dog wagged his tail, flopped down by the fire, and chomped noisily on the bone.

When it was gone, Dog ran to the Woman. "I've never eaten a bone so meaty," he said. "I'd give anything to lie by a warm fire and chew bones like this forever."

Woman smiled. "You can chew delicious, meaty bones forever. Man has gone hunting, but he needs help. If you'll hunt with Man during the day and guard our home at night, we'll give you all the bones from our stew."

Dog barked and jumped up to lick Woman's face.

"He's so eager to please, he's nearly wagging himself in half," said Cat. He raised his back and stretched his claws. "Foolish Dog. I would never give up my freedom to live in a house. I am a Cat, and I walk by myself."

Horse, Cow, and Cat saw Dog bound off to help Man hunt every morning. They watched him guard the house every night. They saw Woman scratch Dog's head and throw sticks for Dog to retrieve. They watched Dog lie by the fire in the cave, chewing bone after bone.

"Dog looks happy," said Cow.

"Dog has traded his freedom for sticks and bones," said Cat.

"He doesn't look as if he minds," said Horse. "I'm going down to see if Dog likes his new life. Do you want to come along?"

"Heavens, no," said Cow. "I'd be much too afraid."

"No, thank you," said Cat. "I am a Cat, and I walk by myself." Cat stretched out on a rock and pretended to sun himself.

Horse trotted down to the house. Cat waited till Horse could no longer see him, then turned and followed him quietly through the woods.

Woman had just returned from the field with a pile of newly dried hay. Cat saw Woman lead Horse to the pile. He watched Horse happily chomp fresh hay all morning.

When Woman came out of the house with a braided halter, Horse said, "I've never tasted hay so crisp and fragrant. I'd give anything to eat fresh hay like this forever."

Woman smiled. "You can eat fresh hay forever. If you'll help us plant our food and carry it home when it's harvested, we'll give you as much hay as you like."

Horse whinnied and stamped his front hoof with joy. He lowered his head so that Woman could slide the braided halter over his nose.

Cat hissed angrily at what he saw. "Foolish Horse," he said. "I would never give up my freedom to live in a house. I am a Cat, and I walk by myself."

Cow and Cat watched Horse as he plowed the fields and then carried the harvest. They saw Man scratch Horse's head and rub his nose. They saw Horse eat an apple from Woman's hand each morning, and feast on freshly dried hay each afternoon.

"Horse looks happy," said Cow.

"Horse has traded his freedom for a pile of hay," said Cat.

Cow watched Horse day after day, until finally her curiosity was stronger than her fear. "I'm going down to see if Horse likes his new life. Do you want to come along?"

"No," Cat yawned. "I am a Cat, and I walk by myself." Cat pretended to slip off into the woods to hunt.

Cow ambled down to the stone house. Cat turned and followed her quietly through the forest.

Cat saw Woman lead Cow to a patch of grass and clover near the house. He watched as Cow spent the morning happily munching the fresh grass and sweet clover.

When Woman came out of the house with a braided rope, Cow said, "I've never tasted grass so fresh or clover so sweet. I'd give anything to stay here forever."

Woman smiled. "You can stay here forever. If you will give us warm milk each morning, you may stay in this clover patch as long as you like."

Cow flicked her tail with joy. She lowered her head so that Woman could loop the braided rope around her neck.

Cat yowled, "Foolish Cow." He stalked away. "I would never give up my freedom to live in a house. I am a Cat, and I walk by myself."

The forest was lonely now that Cow was gone. Cat perched on a high branch where he had a good view of the stone house.

Cat watched Woman milk Cow. He saw Woman pat Cow's side and scratch Cow's head. He saw Cow nibble grain from Man's hand every morning and graze in the clover field every afternoon.

"It looks like a good life," said Cat. "But Cow has traded her freedom for a patch of clover." Cat sharpened his claws on the bark of a tree and pretended not to notice how happy Cow looked.

The aroma of fresh, warm milk drifted up from the house. Cat sniffed. "Perhaps I'll wander down there," he said, "and see how long it takes for Dog, Horse, and Cow to tire of their new life with Woman and Man."

Woman saw Cat approach the house. "You could come inside and live," said Woman, "if you had something to trade for it."

"I'll never give up my freedom for a house," said Cat.

Woman watched Cat stretch out near the entrance, trying to feel the warmth of the fire. "You could lie close to the fire," said Woman, "if you had something to trade for it."

"I'll never give up my freedom for a fire," said Cat.

Woman noticed Cat's whiskers twitching as he sniffed the warm milk. "You could have milk three times a day," said Woman, "that is, if you had something to trade for it."

"I'll never give up my freedom for milk," said Cat. "I am a Cat, and I walk by myself. But I would certainly accept a gift if a beautiful woman were to offer me a bowl of milk."

Woman had to spend most of her days in the house by herself while Man was out hunting, so she was flattered when Cat called her beautiful.

"You don't have anything to trade for a dry house," she told Cat, "and I can't think of any reason to compliment you, but if I ever praise you as you have praised me, I'll let you live here with us. You can lie by the fire, and I'll give you milk three times a day."

Cat stretched and pretended not to be interested in Woman's bargain, but he watched the house, looking for an opportunity to be praised.

Soon a mouse scampered across the ground.

"Not again," moaned Woman. "How can I keep these creatures out?"

"Easily," said Cat. He chased the mouse and devoured it.

"You're more useful than I thought," Woman said as she smiled, "which means I've praised you."

From that day on, Cat lived in the stone house along with Dog, Horse, and Cow. Every day, Dog went hunting with Man, Horse plowed the fields, and Cow gave Woman warm milk. Dog, Horse, and Cow never talked about being wild. In fact, they had forgotten what their wild, free lives were like.

Cat was the only one who still acted a bit wild. He spent his days in the house, lying by the fire and drinking warm milk. Man and Woman scratched Cat's head and stroked his fur. In return, Cat kept the house free of mice.

But at night Cat would disappear from the house to do those wild things only wild cats know about. He left when he chose and came back when he decided it was time.

"I get along quite well with the humans, and I like living with them in the house," he said, "but still, I am a Cat, and I walk by myself."

The Brave Little Tailor

Adapted by Jennifer Boudart
Illustrated by Jeremy Tugeau

One morning, a little tailor sat in his shop. He bent over his work, sewing as he always did this time of day. Suddenly the tailor had a taste for jelly. He took out a loaf of bread, and cut a big slice from it. The tailor licked his lips as he spread on some jelly. "I am more hungry than I thought," he told himself. "Let's hope this jelly fills my belly and clears my head."

The tailor wanted to sew a few more stitches before eating his snack. When he finished, he saw a swarm of flies buzzing around his tasty jelly. The little man waved the flies away with his hand. But they flew right back.

The tailor grabbed a scrap of cloth and growled, "Now I'll let you have it!" The cloth burst through the air as the tailor beat at the buzzing flies.

When he lifted the cloth away, seven flies lay dead on the table. "The whole world should know of my skill!" said the tailor. He cut a belt just his size. With his finest thread, he sewed these words: "Seven in one blow!" The tailor tied the red belt around his waist. "I feel the need for a big adventure," he shouted.

The tailor looked for something useful to take with him on his big adventure. All he found was an old piece of cheese. He put it in his pocket. As he was locking the door, he heard a rustle in the bushes. A bird was trapped among the thorns. The tailor gently pulled the bird from the bush. He put it in his pocket with the cheese. Then he began his adventure.

The tailor walked through town and up the side of a mountain without stopping. At the top, he met a giant. "Hello, Giant," said the tailor with a bow. "I am on a big adventure. Will you join me?"

"A little man like you on a big adventure?" rumbled the giant. For an answer, the tailor showed the giant his belt. The giant read the words: "Seven in one blow!"

The giant found it very hard to believe that this tiny tailor could kill seven men with one blow. So he decided to test the little man's strength. "Can you do this?" asked the giant. He picked up a stone and squeezed it until water dripped from the stone.

"Watch this," the tailor said as he took something from his pocket. The giant thought it was a stone, too, but it was actually the piece of cheese. The tailor squeezed it until liquid whey dripped from his hand.

The giant raised his eyebrows. "Well, can you do this?" he asked. He picked up another stone and tossed it high into the air. It flew almost out of sight.

"Watch this," the tailor said as he took something from his pocket. It was the bird, of course. With a toss of his hand, the tailor sent the little bird flying out of sight.

The giant was a poor loser. "Perhaps you would like to come home with me and meet my friends," the giant said with an evil gleam in his eye.

"Certainly," the tailor replied.

The giant took the tailor to his cave. A group of giants sat around a roaring fire. They watched as their friend led the little man to a bed. "You can sleep here," said the giant. "Even a man who can kill seven in one blow needs to rest!"

The tailor was not used to such a big bed. So he slept in a corner instead. It was good for him that he did. During the night, the giants pounded on the bed with clubs, until they thought they had taken care of the pesky tailor.

In the morning, the giants went swimming in the river. They joked about the strange man and his silly belt. When the tailor walked up whistling a merry tune, the giants were so afraid, they ran away without their clothes! The tailor laughed and left the giants behind. He walked very far and then lay down for a nap on a soft, grassy hill.

The tailor slept a long time. Some people found him and read his belt. They thought he was a mighty soldier. When the tailor awoke, the people took him to meet their king.

The king had never met a man who could kill seven in one blow. He hired the stranger for his army, and gave him a bag full of gold.

The other soldiers were very angry. "This is not fair, Your Highness! We will leave your army if we don't get a bag full of gold, too."

The king could not lose a whole army over one man. He decided to get rid of his new soldier. So he went to the little man with a challenge. "I need you to kill two giants that live in my woods. If you do, I will give you my daughter and half my kingdom as a reward." The tailor knew this was his chance to become a hero.

The tailor went into the woods the next morning. One hundred soldiers went with him. As he rode, the tailor made a plan. "Stay behind until I call you," he told the soldiers.

Then he rode on until he found the two giants asleep under a tree. The tailor climbed the tree. He began dropping acorns on one giant's head. The giant awoke and turned to his friend. "Why did you wake me by thumping my head?" roared the giant. Before his friend could answer, the angry giant threw an acorn at him.

The two giants fought each other until both fell dead to the ground. The tailor called the king's soldiers to come and see what he had done. They were amazed. The new soldier had beaten the giants without getting a scratch! "Two giants are easy compared to killing seven in one blow," laughed the tailor.

The king heard about the tailor's great feat, but he was not ready to give up his daughter and half his riches, yet. So he thought of a plan. "Brave soldier, a wild boar is tearing up the farmers' crops," explained the king. "Please catch it for me."

Off the tailor went to find the boar. He was not sure how he would catch it, but he knew he would think of something. Suddenly he heard a snort behind him. The boar was coming his way! The tailor ran into a barn. The boar was close behind. The little man crawled out a window just as the boar came through the doors. The tailor ran to shut the doors. The animal was trapped!

When the king asked how he had tricked the beast, the proud tailor said, "One who can kill seven in one blow can surely get a silly boar to do what he wants!"

The king tried one last trick to get rid of the tailor. He ordered the little man to catch the unicorn that was scaring the villagers. The tailor agreed to go, but only if he could go alone. The king agreed. So the tailor walked into the woods, looking for the unicorn.

When the tailor heard a crashing sound, he turned to see the unicorn running straight for him. The tailor stood perfectly still. Just as the unicorn reached him, the tailor jumped out of the way. He had been standing in front of a tree. The unicorn's horn drove deep into the tree and became stuck in the hard wood.

The tailor freed the unicorn and rode it back to the palace in a cloud of dust. Again the king was amazed to see the tailor. "How did you tame this wild unicorn?" he asked the tailor.

The tailor told the king, "For one who has killed seven in one blow, a unicorn is like a kitten!"

The king had no choice but to keep his promise to the tailor. He ordered his servants to plan a large feast. The tailor and the king's daughter were wed in a ceremony that was attended by everyone in the kingdom.

The king thought his new son-in-law was a hero. He did not know that the man who married his daughter and took half his kingdom was only a simple tailor.

The tailor almost gave up his secret one night. His wife heard him say in his sleep, "Boy, make me that waistcoat and patch that gown, or there will be trouble!"

The princess ran to her father. "He is not a hero, Father! He is only a tailor," she cried.

"Daughter, leave your door open tonight," said the king. "My soldiers will sneak in and take care of that little man once and for all. You should not be married to a simple tailor."

The king's waterbearer heard the king talking about the tailor. He thought highly of the tailor for his courage and skill, so he ran to tell the tailor about the king's plan.

That night, the tailor pretended to fall asleep. He groaned and then whispered, "Boy, make me that waistcoat and patch that gown or there will be trouble. I have killed seven at one blow, beaten two giants, trapped a boar, and tamed a wild unicorn. I am not afraid to make trouble . . . even with soldiers outside my door." The soldiers heard this and ran in fear. That is how a simple man's bravery and brains made him a hero.

George Washington and the Cherry Tree

Adapted by Catherine McCafferty
Illustrated by Jerry Harston

Many stories and books have been written about George Washington. When the American colonies fought for their freedom, Washington led the soldiers against the British. When the brand-new country needed a leader, Washington served as its first president.

The legend of George Washington's honesty is just as famous as these true stories of bravery. It is called a legend, because no one has any records to say that the story really happened. Did young George Washington chop down a cherry tree? Maybe not. But this story shows just how important it is for everyone to tell the truth.

What a fine day it was for young George Washington! At just six years old, he had his very own hatchet. George was proud of his new hatchet. It felt solid in his small hands. Its blade was shiny and sharp. George swung the hatchet through the air just to see the sun shine on it.

His father stopped him. "A hatchet is not a toy, George," his father warned. "It can do much harm if you are not careful. Always take care when you use it."

George nodded at his father's words. His father was talking to him like a man. Owning a hatchet was a serious thing, indeed. George promised he would always be very careful with it.

Once he was outside, though, George felt more excited than serious. His family's farm seemed full of things that needed cutting. George tested his hatchet on a row of weeds at the edge of the cornfield. It sliced through their thin stems. The row of tall weeds became a pile of cut weeds. George smiled. He took aim at the thicker stalks of the corn plants.

Whack! Three cornstalks fell with a rustle and a crunch. George stepped back, startled. He looked at his hatchet with a new respect. His father was right. He would have to be careful. Then George saw that an ear of corn had fallen to the ground. It was even thicker than the cornstalks. George's hatchet sliced the corncob in half.

Not far from the cornfield, George's father tended to his fruit trees. He was proud of the sweet apples, peaches, and pears that the trees gave his family. He kept the trees' branches trimmed, and watched them for any sign of sickness. Mr. Washington gave extra attention to his youngest tree. It was a cherry tree, and it had come from far away. The cherry tree had been just a sapling when Mr. Washington planted it. Each year, Mr. Washington watched it grow stronger. This year, there were blossoms on its branches. Perhaps, he thought, it might even give fruit. Mr. Washington thought of the fresh cherries they could pick. Then he thought of the cherry pies Mrs. Washington could bake with the sweet cherries. He smiled and gave the cherry tree a pat.

George ran up to Mr. Washington as he walked back to the house for supper. "This hatchet works well, Father," he said.

His father smiled. "Yes, I've seen you using it."

When they sat down for dinner, George laid his hatchet down in a corner of the room. All through dinner, he looked over at it. What could he do with it next?

George thought about going into the woods and chopping down tree after tree. Then he thought about chopping the fallen trees into smaller pieces to be used in the fire. "I would be so useful," George thought.

George's mother noticed how George watched the hatchet. "I think it's time you put that hatchet to good use, George," she said. "Tomorrow, I would like you to chop up kindling for the fire."

"Oh yes, Mother!" George said. "I can start tonight!"

Mrs. Washington shook her head. "You'll do better work after a good night's sleep."

George put his hatchet under his bed. He climbed into bed and closed his eyes. After a few minutes, he leaned over the side of the bed and peeked at the floor. The hatchet was still there. George had a hard time falling asleep. He couldn't wait until morning. He saw himself chopping piles, and then mounds, and then mountains of kindling! Why, he would chop enough kindling to keep the kitchen fires burning for years! When George finally fell asleep, he dreamed that he was a great woodcutter. With one sweep of his hatchet, he cut down whole forests.

The next morning, George hurried through his breakfast. As soon as he finished his last bite, he told his mother, "I'm ready to chop kindling now." His mother sent him outside to the woodshed. George looked around for the kindling. It was not a mountain of kindling. And it was barely a mound. Still, George went to work. He chopped the long, thin branches into small sticks.

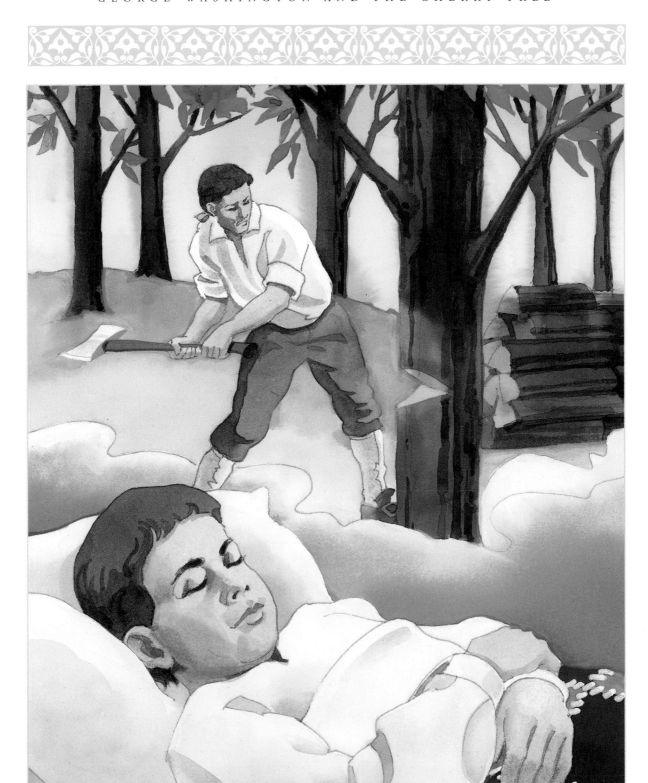

Then George chopped the small sticks into smaller sticks. Then he chopped the smaller sticks into pieces. George saw that the pieces were too small to be chopped further. He ran inside to tell his mother that he had finished his job.

"Is there any more kindling for me to chop, Mother?" George asked.

"No, George. You may play for a while," she said.

George didn't want to play. He wanted to use his hatchet. He thought of the cornstalks and the corncob he had cut yesterday. Then he tried to think of something else to cut.

"Mother," he said, "would you like me to chop some logs for the fire?"

Mrs. Washington smiled. "No, George. Those logs would be much too big for your hatchet to cut."

George wandered outside. Just how much could his hatchet cut? The kindling had been easy. It was so thin. The cornstalks and the corncob were thicker, but they had been easy to cut, too. George decided to test his hatchet again. He went to an old, thick fence post. On the first strike, his hatchet's blade sunk deep into the wood. George had to tug to pull it free. "Well, that was too thick," George thought. George looked around for something thicker than the cornstalks but thinner than the fence post. Then he spotted the trunk of the young cherry tree.

The tree trunk looked just right. It wasn't full-grown as the apple and pear trees were. George chopped at the cherry tree. The blade dug into the tree trunk, but pulled free easily. Why, it would take just a few strokes of his hatchet to cut the tree down! George chopped until the tree fell. George looked proudly at the fallen tree. Then he remembered how much his father liked the cherry tree. And he remembered how his father had told him to be careful with the hatchet.

George hurried back to the woodshed. He sat in a dark corner. If only he had been careful, as his father had told him!

Mr. Washington saw the fallen tree on his way to the house. He saw that its trunk was cut through with many strokes. Then he realized there would be no cherries. There would be no cherry pies. After all his hard work and care, there would be no cherry tree. George's father sadly walked back to the house.

George saw his father go past the woodshed. Slowly, he followed his father into the house. He carried the hatchet with him.

His father turned as he heard George come in the door. He looked at George. He looked at George's hatchet. George could see that his father was very angry.

"George," his father said, "do you know who killed my cherry tree?"

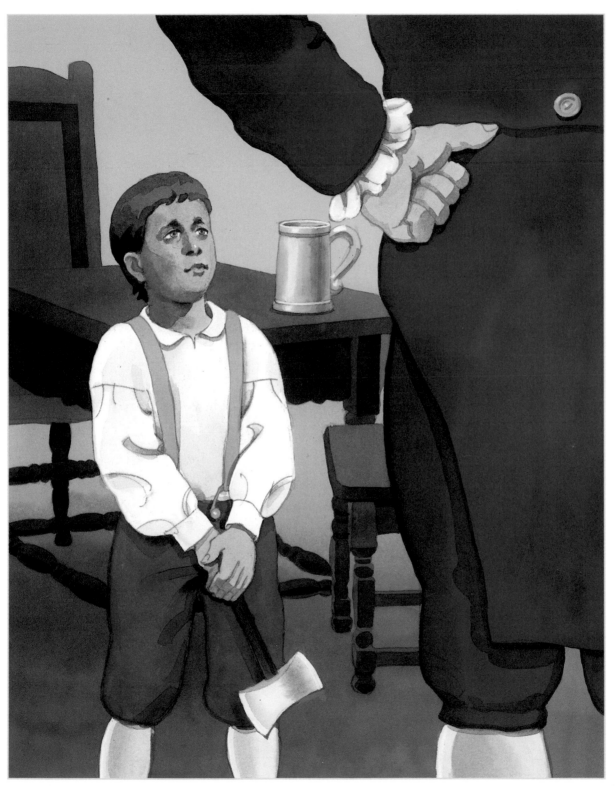

George took a deep breath. He tried not to think about how he would be punished. Instead George said, "I cannot tell a lie, Father. I cut down your cherry tree." George looked at his feet. He felt like crying, but he said, "I wasn't careful with the hatchet. I'm sorry, Father." Then he waited to hear what his punishment would be.

George felt his father's hands on his shoulders. "Look at me, Son," said Mr. Washington. George made himself look up at his father. To George's surprise, his father no longer seemed angry. In fact, Mr. Washington looked rather calm.

"You have been honest, Son," said Mr. Washington. "That means more to me than any cherry tree ever could."

Of course, George's father was disappointed that there would be no cherries to make cherry pies, but he also wanted to reward his son for telling the truth. George did something terribly wrong, but he wasn't punished, because he also did something right. "So remember, you must always tell the truth," George's father added.

George never forgot his father's words. They were a lesson for life.

The Wild Swans

Adapted by Brian Conway
Illustrated by Kathy Mitchell

Once there was a king who had happiness and great fortune. Of all his treasures, he was proudest of his four children, the most perfect children in the land. His three fine, strong sons would do anything for their father, and the king's greatest joy, his daughter Elise, was clearly the dearest, sweetest, and most beautiful child in all the world.

Elise spent much of her time in her garden. Next to her brothers and her father, her lovely roses were Elise's greatest treasures. She would spend hour after hour caring for them.

Then one day the king hurried to find Elise. He was very worried. "I have terrible news," he told her. "You are in danger."

The king had many treasures, it is true, but for this he also had many wicked and powerful enemies. They were evil sorcerers and magicians who believed no one should have as much happiness as the king did.

"I fear for your safety," the king told his daughter. "You must go away from me now."

"But, Father," Elise sobbed, "I want to stay with you and my brothers."

The king sighed. "Your brothers have been taken away from us," he sadly told her. "I know not where. I cannot stand to lose you, too."

The king told the sweet princess to go with his trusted servants, who would take her to safety in their home in the forest. He said he might never see her again.

"When you're old enough," said the king, "find your brothers and come back to me."

He kissed her good-bye. Elise did as her father said. She lived hidden away in the servants' house for many years. She was treated well, but she was very unhappy. Elise longed to see her three beloved brothers again.

When Elise was old enough, she set off in search of her brothers. She had no idea where to look, but she knew in her heart they were still alive, and something inside told her they needed her help.

After several days of wandering and hoping for some sign, Elise met an old woman picking berries in the forest.

"I am looking for my three brothers," Elise told the woman. "They are fine, strong princes. Have you seen them?"

"I have seen nothing all day but three white swans with golden crowns on their heads," the old woman replied. "They were sunning themselves on the shore."

She directed Elise to the spot. There, Elisc found three white feathers. She clutched them close to her and fell asleep while she waited for the swans to return.

Just before sunset, Elise woke up to see three majestic swans gliding down to the shore. They landed beside her, and, as the last ray of sunshine disappeared over the sea, the three swans changed magically into three princes. Elise was overjoyed to see her brothers again. They held her close and told her what had happened to them.

On that day many years ago, an evil sorcerer had come to the castle. He found Elise's brothers in the stables. This sorcerer vowed to ruin the king's happiness, which he did the moment he turned the three princes into swans. They had lived apart from their father since then as swans during the day. At nightfall the soft rays of moonlight made them human again. The sorcerer had planned to cast a spell on Elise, too, but gratefully she had escaped.

"We have looked for you," the eldest brother told Elise. "But you were very well hidden."

"We have flown to see our father," the second brother told Elise. "He is safe, but terribly unhappy. He now serves the sorcerer."

"He cannot help us," added the third brother. "But each day he makes a wish on a dried rosebud. He wishes we will find each other and make things right again."

Elise promised to help free her brothers from the sorcerer's wicked spell. Her brothers told her of an enchanted land far across the sea where they might find a way to break the spell.

"Take me with you," Elise urged them. "I know I can help you."

Her brothers prepared a net to carry their sister in. The next morning the sun's rays turned them into swans again. They flew high above the sea, carrying Elise as she slept. Their journey was difficult. They rushed to reach land by nightfall, or else all three brothers and their sister would drop into the sea and be lost forever.

After two days' flight, they arrived at the kingdom across the sea. It was a beautiful kingdom of goodness and kindness. It was said that the Fairy Queen Morgana lived there. Surely she would know how to help them.

Elise's brothers found her a cave to rest in while they searched for Morgana from the skies. As Elise fell asleep there, she wished for a way to free her brothers from the spell. Even in her dreams, Elise prayed for help.

That night Morgana came to Elise in a dream. Elise knew her! She was the woman who Elise had seen picking berries in the woods just a few days before.

"Only you can free your brothers," Morgana whispered to Elise. "But you must sacrifice greatly."

"I will," Elise promised. Then she listened carefully to the Fairy Queen's instructions. "Take the things you treasure most," Morgana said, "and craft three shirts, one for each brother. This may take a very long time, but when you cover the swans with them, the spell will forever be broken."

"There is one more thing," Morgana added. "You may not speak until the shirts are made. If you do, your words will pierce your brothers' hearts like arrows."

With that Morgana disappeared. Elise awoke with a start to find the cave in which she slept was surrounded with hundreds of lovely rosebushes, like the ones she'd had as a child.

She touched the roses. Yes, they were real. She was no longer dreaming. Elise set to work immediately, as Morgana had directed. Though it pained her to destroy their loveliness, Elise picked rose after rose and plucked petal after petal. She used the roses' prickly thorns as needles to string the petals together.

Elise worked tirelessly, day and night. Her brothers visited her there at the cave. Elise didn't dare speak to tell them what she was doing. They cried for her pain and understood that she worked to help them.

After ten days and nights without rest, Elise had finished one shirt. Without pausing, she started again on the second. In ten more days' time she finished the second and began work on the third shirt. Elise was tired, but the thought of freeing her brothers gave her extraordinary strength.

On the thirtieth day, Elise was nearly through with the third shirt. She had one sleeve left to sew. But that day a woodcutter and his wife came upon Elise's rose garden.

"Here are the roses I told you about, my dear," the woodcutter called to his wife. "They sprung up over night."

Her eyes grew large. The woodcutter's wife loved roses, too. She leaned forward for a closer look, and saw Elise working there among the soft piles of petals.

"What are you doing in the woods alone?" they asked, but Elise didn't dare speak, out of fear for her brothers' lives. "Poor child, come with us. We'll give you proper food and rest."

Elise struggled against the woodcutter. She was grateful, but she could not speak to tell them why she resisted. She thought only of her brothers.

Elise did not want to leave her new rose garden. She wanted to finish the third shirt, and she needed the roses to do it.

Elise finally gathered up the shirts and as many roses as she could carry. Then she went sadly with the woodcutter and his wife. They walked many miles to their house. Elise feared she would never see her rose garden again.

"We'll make a proper girl out of you," the woodcutter said.

Elise stayed there for many days and did as the woodcutter and his wife asked. At night, though, she would stay awake to sew the last shirt. Before long, Elise ran out of rose petals. She needed at least one more blooming rosebush to finish the shirt.

The next day Elise found what she needed in the woodcutter's garden. There his wife kept her prized roses. Elise crept out of the house that night and plucked the petals from the roses, then began sewing. At sunrise, she had one cuff left to sew as the woodcutter's wife stormed into the garden.

"Ungrateful girl!" she shouted. "You've ruined my roses!"

Flying the skies in search of some sign of their sister, Elise's brothers heard the shouts of the woodcutter's wife.

They flew to the house and landed in the garden. They squawked at the woodcutter, who ran in fear for his bow. Elise quickly spread the three shirts over the swans.

The rose petals ruffled in a warm swirling breeze. Before her eyes, the swans became men again, filling the shirts Elise had made with love and sacrifice for them alone.

Elise ran to her brothers' arms. The youngest brother, who wore the unfinished shirt, still had some feathers on one arm, but he did not mind.

Elise, anxious to speak now that the spell had been broken, explained everything to the woodcutter and his wife. "I'm sorry that I have been so difficult, when you have been so kind," said Elise. "My brothers and I thank you. We will repay you this moment."

Elise and her brothers brought all the rosebushes from the forest cave and planted them in the garden behind the woodcutter's house. Elise and her brothers sent for their father the very next day. A flock of ten wild swans delivered a message of joy. The king now had the strength and desire to escape the evil sorcerer. He journeyed by ship to the family's new home.

Reunited, the happy family thrived again. Elise and her brothers prepared a new castle for their father, who became the king of a new land.

Of course, Elise's brothers remembered to plant a rose garden on the castle grounds. It is said that this rose garden is where Elise weaves the most fragrant and lovely rosebushes by hand and sends a flock of wild swans to plant them in forests all over the world.

Rikki-Tikki-Tavi

Adapted by Pegeen Hopkins
Illustrated by Richard Bernal

This is the tale of a brave mongoose, named Rikki-tikki-tavi, and his great fight to help a family that saved him. It all started and ended in the far-off land of India. It began on the first sunny day after many days of darkness and rain. A young English boy, Teddy, went outside to explore. There he found a mongoose in the road.

A mongoose is a small animal, a bit like a cat and a bit like a weasel. This mongoose, Rikki-tikki, had thick hair and a bushy tail that made him look like a cat. His skinny head and the way he moved his feet, though, were just like a weasel. Both his wiggly nose and his little eyes were pink. But when Rikki-tikki got mad, his eyes turned deep, deep red.

A big summer flood had washed Rikki-tikki out of the hole where he lived. The water carried him along and dumped him in a ditch just outside Teddy's house.

"Look, Mommy, a dead mongoose," Teddy said as he carried Rikki-tikki inside. "Let's have a funeral."

"No, Teddy," said his mother. "Maybe he's just wet. Why don't we dry him off?"

Teddy's father wrapped him in a towel to warm him up. The towel tickled Rikki-tikki's little pink nose. "Ah-choo!" The mongoose sneezed and then looked around. Rikki-tikki, like all mongooses, was very curious.

Rikki-tikki ran up to Teddy and rubbed his wet head under the boy's chin. "Hey, that tickles," Teddy cried.

"He wants to be your friend," Teddy's father laughed.

"Wow, I can't believe it," said Teddy's mother. "He's a wild animal. I guess he's so tame because we've been kind to him."

"As long as we don't pick him up by the tail, or put him in a cage," said Teddy's father, "he'll run in and out of the house all day. You'll see."

Then Rikki-tikki scurried off. He spent the whole day running through Teddy's house.

First he went for a swim in the family's bathtub. Then he dirtied his nose, sniffing the ink in an inkwell. Later he burnt his nose while bumping it against Teddy's father's cigar. But at bedtime, he climbed up into bed right next to Teddy.

"Is that safe?" Teddy's mother asked. "What if Rikki-tikki bites or scratches Teddy?"

"He won't do that," Teddy's father replied. "Teddy is safer with him than if he had a guard dog watching over him. But if a snake were to come in here. . ."

Teddy's mother interrupted him. "Don't even say that," she said. They turned out the light. Teddy and Rikki-tikki went straight to sleep.

The next morning Rikki-tikki went out into the big garden at the back of the house to look around. It was a large yard with rosebushes as big as people. It had lime trees and orange trees, bunches of bamboo, and plenty of tall grass.

Rikki-tikki heard a sad song coming from the trees. He looked up and saw Darzee, the songbird, and his wife. One of their eggs had fallen out of their nest and a snake had come along and eaten it. "Those snakes, Nag and Nagaina, are evil," Darzee cried. They weren't just any snakes. They were cobras, which are some of the biggest and deadliest snakes around.

"I'm sorry," said Rikki-tikki, "but I am new here. Who is Nag?"

Just then, a big black snake slithered up through the tall grass. It hissed a low breath that was cold and harsh like steam whistling out of a radiator. Rikki-tikki was so scared by the sound that he jumped back two feet.

The snake, five feet long from the tip of his tongue to the back of his tail, raised his head and its hooded back. He stared at Rikki-tikki with evil eyes that never blinked.

"Who is Nag? I am Nag. I am a cobra, and my family has been ruling this garden for thousands of years. Look at me and be afraid."

Rikki-tikki was scared for a minute, but no more than that. He knew that as a mongoose, he was supposed to fight snakes. Nag knew it, too.

"Look out!" yelled Darzee's wife. At just that moment, another snake struck at Rikki-tikki from behind. He jumped high in the air as if he was bouncing on a trampoline. The snake, Nag's wife Nagaina, had tried to bite Rikki-tikki. She missed him by inches. Since a cobra bite can be deadly, Rikki-tikki was lucky.

Then, without a word, the two snakes quickly slithered off into the grass. Rikki-tikki went back to the house to see Teddy.

Later that night, Rikki-tikki listened to a peculiar sound. The house was silent, but Rikki-tikki could make out what seemed like the sound of snake skin rubbing on bricks. Nag or Nagaina was in the house! They had come in through the drain in the tub.

As quick as he could, Rikki-tikki ran off to Teddy's parent's bathroom. There he heard two voices whispering in the dark. It was Nag and Nagaina.

"When the house is empty of people," Nagaina was saying, "Rikki-tikki will have to go away. Then the garden will be all ours again. So long as the house is empty, we are the king and queen of the garden. Remember, our eggs in the melon patch will be hatching soon."

"Go in quickly," she said, "and scare off the people. Then you and I will take care of Rikki-tikki together."

Rikki-tikki's eyes glowed the deep red of a polished ruby. He watched as Nag's head came through the drain. He heard Nagaina slide away into the grass outside.

It seemed that Nag intended to wait in the drain until morning. Then the cobra could surprise Teddy's father when he got in the shower, scaring the man and his family away.

Rikki-tikki waited, too. He thought of all the nice things that Teddy's family had done for him. After an hour, he inched closer to the deadly snake. He would fight the snake and send him away for good. But he had to make sure that he bit the snake in just the right spot.

Then without warning and as quick as a flash of lightning, Rikki-tikki jumped. He grabbed the snake by the back of the neck. Nag whipped his hooded head around. The snake swung Rikki-tikki like a limp rag doll. Still, Rikki-tikki held tight.

Then Rikki-tikki felt a burst of wind over his shoulder. He heard a large crack. Teddy's father had taken a large stick and hit Nag in the head. The black cobra lay still on the cold tile floor. Teddy's father quickly picked up the snake and got rid of him.

"Oh my," Teddy's mother cried from the bathroom doorway. "That mongoose has saved all our lives."

Rikki-tikki walked back into Teddy's room and spent the rest of the night there. When morning came, he knew he would have to find Nagaina and fight her, too. Once she found out that Nag was gone, she would be very angry. She would be very dangerous . . . to everyone.

Rikki-tikki went to the garden with a plan. "Darzee," he called to the songbird, "you have to help me. You must distract Nagaina while I go find her eggs."

Mrs. Darzee agreed to run over to where the black snake was lying in the grass and lure her away. Nagaina was sitting by the house and crying over her lost Nag.

"Oh no," exclaimed Mrs. Darzee so the snake could hear, "my wing has been broken and I can't fly." The bird, of course, was fine. She just needed to get the snake away from her eggs. Then Rikki-tikki could snatch them. As the bird fluttered down the garden path, Nagaina followed close behind.

When he saw them pass by, Rikki-tikki ran over to the melon patch and began carrying off the eggs he found. He had just come back for the last egg, when Mrs. Darzee flew over to him.

"Oh Rikki-tikki, Nagaina has trapped Teddy and his parents on the porch of the house."

Rikki-tikki ran as fast as his legs could carry him. He reached the porch with the last of Nagaina's eggs in his mouth. Teddy's family had sat down to eat, but none of them moved. Their faces were as white as snow.

Nagaina stood inches away from Teddy's chair. She was ready to strike at any moment.

Rikki-tikki dropped the egg on the floorboard. He yelled, "Nagaina, I have the last of your eggs here. I have taken all the others from the garden. This is your last one. Leave them alone, and I will give this egg to you."

Nagaina spun around. She forgot everything for the sake of that one egg. As soon as she turned away from them, Teddy's father grabbed him and pulled him to safety.

Now Nagaina turned on Rikki-tikki, and a wicked fight began. The two animals moved round and round in an angry dance on the porch. But Rikki-tikki was very quick. He jumped back with each of Nagaina's wicked strikes.

Rikki-tikki forgot about the egg, though. After a few minutes, Nagaina got close to her treasure. Before Rikki-tikki could catch her, she snapped up the egg in her mouth and raced down the steps.

Rikki-tikki followed behind her, right on her tail. Over the garden paths they went: snake, egg, and mongoose. Mrs. Darzee flew straight at the snake, hoping to slow her down a bit. She gave Rikki-tikki the chance to grab hold of Nagaina's tail. Rikki-tikki bit down just as Nagaina slid down into her hole.

Rikki-tikki went down into the hole with her. They continued the fight. The long grass at the entrance of the hole shook as the two struggled underground. Then the grass stopped waving. All the animals thought Rikki-tikki had lost.

Suddenly, Rikki-tikki's tiny head popped up out of the hole. "Nagaina has taken her egg and gone," he said. "She will never come back to this garden again."

Then he walked off to a sunny patch of grass and fell asleep. The tiny mongoose was content. He owed Teddy's family a big favor for saving him from the flood. By keeping his English friends safe from Nag and Nagaina, Rikki-tikki-tavi had returned the kindness.

The Nightingale

Adapted by Lisa Harkrader
Illustrated by Robin Moro

Many years ago, the emperor of China lived in a palace that was surrounded by beautiful gardens. Visitors came from all over the world to admire his silk draperies, exquisite vases, and rare flowers.

But after the visitors toured the palace and gardens, they wanted to see more. "Don't let our trip end," they would say.

A fisherman heard these words. "I can show you the most beautiful thing in all of China," he would say.

He began leading visitors into the forest to see a beautiful nightingale that lived there. At first the visitors would grumble. "We trudged all the way out here to see a plain gray bird?"

But then the nightingale would open its mouth. Its voice was pure and strong. Its song was lovelier than anything the visitors had ever heard.

The visitors returned home and told their friends about the nightingale's beautiful singing. More people came to visit the palace, the gardens, and the plain gray bird that sang in the forest. The nightingale became known as the most beautiful thing in all of China. Everyone had heard of this remarkable bird.

Everyone, that is, except the emperor himself.

The emperor of China was an old man. He stayed inside his palace and knew nothing of the nightingale's lovely song.

One day the emperor of China received a letter that came from the emperor of Japan.

"I have heard of your wonderful nightingale," the Japanese emperor wrote. "He is the most beautiful thing in all of China. Some people say he is the most beautiful thing in all the world. I will arrive in two days to pay you a visit and admire this heavenly bird."

The emperor of China was puzzled. He summoned his prime minister. "Have you heard of this nightingale that is the most beautiful thing in all of China?" the emperor asked.

"No, Your Excellency." The prime minister scratched his chin. "Your painted screens, or your silver chimes, or your delicate orchids could be the most beautiful things in China. But nightingales are quite plain."

"That may be," said the emperor. "But the emperor of Japan arrives in two days. He expects to see this nightingale. Search until you find it."

The prime minister started in the cellar and ended in the attic. He looked under rugs and behind furniture. He searched every inch of the palace, but he could not find the nightingale.

Now there was only one day left before the Japanese emperor's arrival. The emperor of China was worried. He summoned the prime minister and all the palace guards.

"The emperor of Japan will be here tomorrow," the Chinese emperor told them. "He is expecting to see this nightingale that is the most beautiful thing in all of China. Spread out and search the gardens. The bird must be there somewhere."

The prime minister and the palace guards trooped out into the gardens. They climbed trees and waded through fountains. They turned over rocks and peeked under shrubs. They searched every inch of every garden, but they could not find the nightingale.

The next morning the emperor of China received a message. The Japanese emperor's ship had just sailed into the harbor. The Chinese emperor summoned the prime minister, the palace guards, and all the lords and ladies of the court.

"The emperor of Japan will be here today," he told them. "Spread out into the forest surrounding my gardens. Don't come back until you've found this magnificent nightingale."

The prime minister, the palace guards, and all the lords and ladies of the court trekked into the woods. They shook vines and rustled leaves. They peeked in hollow logs and splashed through streams.

They were about to give up when they came upon the fisherman. He led them to the nightingale.

The prime minister, followed by the guards and all the lords and ladies of the court, marched into the palace as the Japanese emperor arrived.

"So this is the famous nightingale, the most beautiful thing in all of China," said the emperor of Japan. "I must say, he looks rather plain."

The nightingale flew to the windowsill. He opened his mouth. Out came the most beautiful song either of the emperors had ever heard. The emperor of Japan was speechless. The emperor of China cried tears of joy.

The nightingale warbled and trilled until even the prime minister, the palace guards, and all the lords and ladies of the court were weeping.

"I must find a way to thank you for allowing me to hear your nightingale's song," declared the emperor of Japan. "He truly is the most beautiful thing in all of China."

"Your happiness is thanks enough," replied the emperor of China as tears of joy rolled down his cheeks.

The emperor of Japan soon went home to his palace across the sea. Day after day the nightingale's song filled the palace. Day after day someone always said, "Too bad the plain nightingale doesn't look as lovely as he sounds."

The emperor heard these comments and became very angry. The nightingale's song had brought him such joy. He was happier now than he had ever been. "I will not have people saying unkind words about the nightingale," he said.

The emperor gave the nightingale a golden perch to sit on. He adorned the nightingale with ribbons and jewels.

The people of the kingdom were very delighted. "Now the nightingale looks almost as lovely as he sounds," they said.

The ladies of the court tried to gurgle water in their throats, to see if they could sound like the nightingale, too.

Day after day the nightingale sat on his golden perch, wearing his jewels and singing his song. The nightingale was allowed to fly out of his cage only twice a day. The emperor thought the little bird looked tired and a little sad.

At night the emperor invited the nightingale into his private chambers. There were no golden perches or crowds of people to distract the little nightingale or the emperor. When the nightingale was alone with the emperor, he always felt safe. The nightingale perched on the foot of the emperor's bed and sang a song to the emperor that no one else would ever hear.

"Gold and ribbons and jewels do not enhance your lovely voice," said the emperor. "You are the most beautiful thing in all of China when you are yourself, singing your pure, sweet song."

Before falling asleep, the emperor told stories to the nightingale about his days as a young boy in China. The nightingale sang along to the emperor's story.

"I remember when beautiful things were not kept in golden cages," said the emperor. "Why can't people recognize and enjoy your beauty?"

The emperor confessed his worries to the nightingale. He could trust no one else. The lords and ladies of the emperor's court only told him what they thought he wanted to hear, never the truth. The emperor knew the nightingale couldn't speak, but he also knew that the nightingale would be true. The emperor knew he wouldn't have to listen to lies when he was alone with the nightingale.

The emperor drifted off to sleep each night to the sound of the nightingale's pure, sweet song.

One day a messenger arrived with a present from the emperor of Japan. "I hope you enjoy this gift," wrote the Japanese emperor. "It is a small token compared to the great joy you gave me when you allowed me to listen to the nightingale."

The Chinese emperor opened the package. Inside was a replica of the nightingale, encrusted with emeralds, sapphires, and rubies. On its back was a delicately carved key.

The emperor wound the key. The mechanical bird began to sing one of the nightingale's songs. The bird did not sound quite as lovely as the real nightingale, and it only sang one song, over and over. Still, the emperor was pleased.

He ordered a second golden perch to be placed beside the first. "Now you will get some rest," he told the nightingale.

The people were thrilled. "Finally!" they said. "A nightingale that looks as lovely as it sounds."

They didn't notice that the jeweled bird's song was not as sweet as the real nightingale's song. They asked to hear the new nightingale over and over. The people ignored the real nightingale, so he flew home to the forest.

Only one person noticed that the nightingale had gone—the emperor. He missed his friend deeply.

"Perhaps it's for the best," the emperor said. "The nightingale was unhappy singing for crowds of people day after day. He will be happier in the forest."

The people never grew tired of the mechanical bird's song. The emperor closed his eyes and tried to pretend he was hearing the song of the real nightingale.

The mechanical bird played over and over, day after day, until one morning, with a loud twang and a pop, it stopped.

The emperor shook the bird. The prime minister wriggled its key. The bird would not play. They called in the watchmaker.

"A sprung spring," the watchmaker proclaimed. "I'll fix it, but you'll have to handle the bird with care. Only wind it on special occasions."

The emperor was miserable. He'd lost his friend the nightingale, and now he didn't have the mechanical bird to take his place. The emperor grew sick and weak.

The prime minister, the palace guards, and all the lords and ladies of the court tried everything, but nothing could cure the emperor. The old fisherman heard of the emperor's illness and promptly told the nightingale.

The nightingale flew straight to the emperor's chambers. He perched on his bed and began to sing his beautiful song.

The emperor opened his eyes. "You came back," he whispered. Tears of joy streamed down the emperor's cheeks.

The nightingale sang a sweet song for the emperor. Then the two old friends talked late into the night. The emperor sat up in bed and the color returned to his cheeks.

The nightingale loved the emperor because the emperor appreciated him just as he was. The emperor loved the nightingale because the emperor could be honest with him. All day long the prime minister, the palace guards, and all the lords and ladies of the court told the emperor only what they thought he wanted to hear. But in the evenings, the little nightingale only listened and sang.

"It's because of you that I'm feeling better," said the emperor. "Precious jewels cannot match the beauty of your song, and mechanical parts cannot give the friendship that comes from your heart."

From then on, the nightingale freely roamed the forest during the day. Then at night, he sang his beautiful song to the emperor, making him well and lulling him to sleep.

Paul Bunyan

Adapted by Jennifer Boudart
Illustrated by Gino D'Achille

An amazing baby was once born in the state of Maine. Paul Bunyan was like no other baby seen before or since. When he was only two weeks old, he weighed more than 100 pounds! He ate five dozen eggs, ten sacks of potatoes, and a barrel of oatmeal each day, just for breakfast!

Paul's parents loved him very much. They didn't mind paying expensive food bills or ordering custom-made booties in size 200. The real trouble started when Paul was only a year old and he started to crawl. Do you know what happens when a 500-pound baby crawls around? Earthquakes, that's what! The whole town shook with them!

The townspeople rushed to their crumbling town hall and took a vote. The mayor delivered the news to Paul's parents, "We're sorry, but you'll have to take Paul away."

The Bunyans reluctantly hauled their son to a cave deep in the woods. "We'll miss you, Paul," cried Mrs. Bunyan. "But we can't keep you at home. You're just too big!"

Mr. Bunyan handed Paul an ax, a knife, a fishing pole, and some flint rocks to make a fire. "You'll need these, Son," he said and patted Paul's giant knee.

"Good-bye," they said and walked away.

That night, Paul felt scared and lonely for the first time. He was so lonely that he cried giant tears for a month. Soon his giant tears turned into a great river! And he might have drowned himself in his tears if he hadn't heard a flop, flop, flop!

When Paul looked down, he saw a fish jumping in his river of tears. He caught it with his father's fishing pole, he cleaned it with his father's knife, and he cooked it over a fire made with his father's flint stones. Then Paul enjoyed his fish dinner and smiled for the first time in a month.

Paul Bunyan lived in his cave for the next 20 years. He lived off the land, he worked hard, and he grew to have the strength of 50 men.

When Paul awoke on his 21st birthday, he knew something was different. He looked outside his cave to see gusts of blue snow swirling past him! Paul pulled on his warmest clothes and ran outside.

The snow felt cold upon his face. He held out his tongue and tasted the cold, blue snowflakes. Then Paul heard a sound over the wind: "Maa-maa, maa-maa." It sounded like a baby!

Paul rushed through the woods. "Where are you, baby?" he shouted. Suddenly he spotted a blue tail under a giant snowdrift. He pulled on the tail and out came the biggest ox on earth! Except for its white horns, the animal was frozen blue as the snow.

"Maa-maa," rumbled the giant, blue ox. "There, there, Babe," whispered the giant, bearded man. Paul took the ox back to his cave and built a blazing fire. He fell asleep with his arm around the ox and a wish on his lips: "Please, let Babe live."

Sure enough, the next morning, a big, blue tongue licked Paul awake. Babe had thawed out and warmed up! "You're alive!" Paul exclaimed as he hugged Babe. He was so happy to see his new friend.

From that day forward, Paul Bunyan and Babe the Blue Ox were the best of friends. They went everywhere together, and the earth shook with each footstep they took.

Babe grew quick as blue lightning. Paul liked to close his eyes for ten seconds and then see how much Babe had grown. When Babe was finally full-grown, his horns towered over the treetops.

But that blue ox was just as gentle as he was big. He would do anything for his friend Paul.

Paul loved the deep, dark forests around his cave. Paul also knew how much people needed the trees that grew there. They used the wood from the trees to build new houses, churches, ships, and barns. So one day, Paul turned to Babe and said, "Friend, we have some work to do."

Paul gave his ax a mighty swing as he turned in a circle. "Tim-ber!" he yelled. One after another, ten trees fell to the ground: thump, thump, thump, thump, thump, thump, thump, thump, thump . . . THUMP! "Let's float these trees downriver to the sawmill," said Paul. He piled the trees on Babe's back, and the friends set off for the Big Onion River.

Since Paul and Babe could cover a whole mile in one step, it took them only a week to travel from Maine to the Big Onion River in Minnesota. Then they floated the logs to a sawmill. That's when Paul decided being a lumberjack was the life for him. He and Babe would travel around the country cutting down trees.

Paul and Babe turned every head when they showed up for their first day of work at a new logging camp. No one had ever seen such a big man or ox before. Of course, Paul wasn't used to seeing people at all. They were so small compared to Paul. So at first, Paul made some mistakes.

When Paul had a terrible cold, he kept working and just used a bedsheet for a handkerchief. "AH-CHOO!" Paul sneezed a terrible sneeze the size of a hurricane, and he forgot to cover his mouth! The loggers grabbed onto tree trunks as they flew through the air.

"Cover your mouth," they yelled, "or we'll end up in China!"

Paul learned quickly, though. He stopped trying to shake hands, he didn't raise his voice above a whisper, and he always watched where he stepped.

Soon, Paul Bunyan and Babe the Blue Ox became the most famous lumberjack team in the land. Wherever they went, trees fell like twigs in the wind. They helped out in other ways, too. Lumberjacks were always trading stories about Paul's good deeds.

"Paul Bunyan went fishing with his bare hands! He grabbed enough fish to keep us fed for weeks!" said the cook.

"Paul Bunyan's ox made us a swimming pool with one scrape of his hoof," said the head lumberjack.

"Paul Bunyan cleared my whole yard of leaves with one breath," said the minister's wife.

Paul's new friends did nice things for him and Babe, too. They made Paul a belt from wagon wheels and rope. They gave him a pine-tree comb. They even sewed tents into booties to keep Babe's feet warm in the winter.

Still, there came a day when Paul turned to Babe and said, "It's time to settle down, my friend." But where should they make their home? Paul closed his eyes and took ten giant steps. When he opened them, he was standing on the banks of the Big Onion River—the perfect place to live!

Paul decided to start his own logging company. First he had to hire a crew. He posted signs across the countryside that advertised his new logging company and his giant blue ox.

Word spread fast through the land. Thousands of men came for the chance to work with Paul Bunyan. He made an announcement to all the men who gathered for the job. "There are only two requirements," he said. "All my loggers must stand more than six feet tall, and they must be able to blow out a campfire with one breath."

About a thousand men fit Paul's requirements, so he hired them all!

The new men could cut thousands of trees in one day. They loaded them on Babe's back, and he took them to the river. The Big Onion River was so full of floating trees, you could walk across it without getting your feet wet.

Paul wanted to make sure his crew ate breakfast every morning, so he built a griddle the size of an ice-skating rink. There, he cooked thousands of flapjacks to fill all his loggers' bellies.

Things went well until the spring of the Great Floods. "The rains are rising up from the ground instead of falling down from the sky!" Paul told Babe. "The other lumberjacks can't get to the trees to do their choppin'!"

Luckily, Paul wasn't just big on heart. He was big on brains, too. He knew just what to do. "Order two thousand umbrellas," shouted Paul.

When the train dropped off the umbrellas, Paul cut off their handles. He showed the crew how to strap the umbrellas onto their feet. The crew floated across the flooded camp and right into the forest. "Ya-hoo!" the men cheered. But Paul would have another problem to solve soon.

The Great Floods also brought a swarm of ten-foot bees. They buzzed throughout the camp, stinging the men. The loggers couldn't leave their bunkhouses to work. Paul ordered a sugar boat to sail up the river. The bees swooped down and followed that sugar boat. They ate so much sugar, they couldn't fly off the deck. The boat sailed away and took the bees to a circus.

"Ya-hoo!" the men cheered again. Paul saved the day!

Paul and Babe floated logs downriver for many years. Each evening Paul took a walk with Babe. They would look out over the land and give thanks for their good fortune. The lumber company is gone, now. What about Paul and Babe? The next time you're in the woods, stop and listen. Maybe you'll hear the far-off sound of "Tim-ber!" on the wind.

The Golden Goose

Adapted by Brian Conway
Illustrated by Karen Dugan

There once was a gentle boy called Samuel. He lived at the edge of the forest with his parents and two older brothers. His family often treated him poorly. They didn't know that he was capable of much greater things, until the day he met a strange old man in the woods.

That day began as Samuel's oldest brother went to cut wood. Their mother packed a nice sweet cake and a bottle of cider for her oldest son to take into the woods. Samuel stayed home and chopped nuts.

In the woods Samuel's brother came upon a little gray man. The man kindly bid him good day and said, "Will you share your cake and cider with a tired old man? I am very hungry and thirsty."

Samuel's brother yelled at the man. "If I give you my food and drink, I won't have enough for myself," he said. "Now get out of my way!"

The brother left the man standing there and went to chop a tree. After a few strong swings, his ax slipped and hit his arm. He suffered a deep cut and could no longer continue his work. The little man saw all this happen. He smiled as Samuel's oldest brother hurried home to dress his wound.

Now the second brother was called to get the firewood. Their mother gave him sweet cake and cider, as she'd done for the oldest brother. Before long the second brother also met up with the old man in the woods. The man kindly bid him good day and said, "Would you share your cake and cider with a tired old man? I am very hungry and thirsty."

This next brother was as selfish as the first. "If I give you my food and drink, I won't have enough for myself," he said. "Now get out of my way!"

The second brother walked away and found a tree to chop. He swung so strongly with his ax, the head of the ax dropped off. It fell firmly on the brother's foot, and he, too, could no longer work. Again the little gray man smiled as he watched Samuel's second brother hobbling home.

Then young Samuel said, "Let me go cut the wood, Father."

"You know nothing about it," his father replied harshly. "But if you are so willing to get hurt, then go."

Samuel's mother handed him some cake and a jug of warm water and sent him on his way. When he reached the forest, Samuel met the little gray man as well. The man kindly bid him good day and said, "Would you share some food and drink with a tired old man? I am very hungry and thirsty."

"I have only stale cake and warm water," Samuel said, "but if you don't mind that, we can eat together."

They sat in the woods to eat. When Samuel reached for their snack, he found a magnificent slice of sweet cake and a large bottle of cider for them to share.

When they finished their tasty meal, the old man told Samuel, "You shared your goods with me, and for that I am grateful. Now you will have good luck to go with your kind heart."

The little gray man pointed at an old tree nearby. "Cut it down and you'll find something special there in its roots." Then the man walked away without another word.

Samuel swiftly cut down the old tree, and when it fell he found a goose sitting among the roots. This was no ordinary goose. Its feathers were made of gold!

Samuel picked up the goose and hurried into town. He had to show this great goose to everyone he knew.

Samuel beamed proudly as he carried his golden goose through town. He passed an inn, and the innkeeper's three curious daughters came out to see the beautiful bird. Each of the three daughters wanted one of the goose's golden feathers to keep for her own.

When Samuel stopped to show off the goose to the three sisters, the oldest sister tiptoed behind Samuel and tugged at the goose's wing. Her hand stuck there so tightly that she could not move it away. She waved to her sisters for their help.

The sisters thought that together they could surely pluck out three gold feathers! They joined hands to pull. Instead, the three sisters found they were all stuck to each other! The sisters hushed their worried squeals and scurried behind Samuel, who never noticed the girls hanging on behind. He marched for the next town to share his goose's beauty with anyone who wished to behold it.

Samuel hurried through a field on his way to the next town. A minister saw the procession and cried, "Have you no shame, girls? Why must you run after the boy? It's just not proper!"

The minister tried to pull the youngest girl away. All too soon he felt that he himself was stuck, and he had to run as fast as his legs could carry him to keep up with the others.

The minister's wife saw her husband running along with the three girls. She cried out in amazement, "Dear Husband, slow down! We have to be at a wedding in a few minutes!"

The minister's wife pulled on his sleeve. Then she was caught up in this silly parade, too.

They passed two farmers on a road. The minister's wife called for help, but as soon as they touched her, the farmers were pulled along, too!

Samuel hurried into the next town, with the curious party of seven behind him.

They reached a town where a king ruled with his only daughter. The young princess was so serious, so solemn that it was believed she could not laugh. So the king sent out a proclamation. Whoever made the princess laugh would have her hand in marriage.

When Samuel heard about the princess, he took his golden goose to her, followed by the three innkeeper's daughters, the minister, the minister's wife, and the two farmers, all running in a row behind him. They quickly walked through town and made their way for the king's castle.

At the sight of this bumbling parade of people, the princess burst into great fits of laughter. She laughed and laughed until the king thought she might not stop.

Samuel asked the laughing princess to marry him, but before she could answer the king stepped in. He did not want Samuel for a son-in-law, so he made up a list of conditions for Samuel.

"First," the king demanded, "you must bring me a man who can drink a whole cellarful of cider."

At once Samuel thought of the little gray man in the woods and rushed away to find him. He found the man looking sad in the same spot as before.

"What is the matter?" Samuel asked.

"It is my thirst," answered the little man. "I cannot seem to quench it. No amount of water will do, and I haven't a drop of good cider."

"Follow me," said Samuel. "You'll soon have enough to drink."

The little gray man happily drank all the cider in the king's cellar, barrel by barrel. Then Samuel approached the king and demanded his bride.

By now the king had a new condition. "Bring me a man who can eat up a mountain of bread," he demanded.

Samuel ran off to find the little gray man, who sat once again in the woods looking forlorn.

"What is the matter?" Samuel asked.

"I am so hungry," said the man. "I feel as though I could eat a mountain of bread."

Samuel smiled and answered, "I believe you shall. Follow me."

And so it was. In just one day, the little man had eaten the whole mountain of bread!

When Samuel approached the king again, the king was ready with a third demand. He thought it would be impossible for Samuel to meet this condition. "Now bring me a ship which sails on land as well as at sea," he mused. "As soon as I see you sail up in it, you can marry my daughter."

Samuel went straight for that spot in the forest. The little man was expecting him. "I have eaten a mountain of bread, and I have drunk a cellarful of cider," said the old man. "And now you shall have a special ship, too. I will share all I have with you, because you have been so kind to me."

The little man brought Samuel a ship which sails on land as well as at sea. Samuel thanked the man, hoisted the sail, and was back at the castle in no time.

The king was astounded but now had no choice. He offered Samuel his daughter's hand.

Samuel took her hand. He asked the princess if she would marry him and share all he had to offer. She smiled so greatly her answer was clear. They were married that day, and, throughout the kingdom, it's said, the princess has never stopped smiling since.

Androcles and the Lion

Adapted by Sarah Toast
Illustrated by Yuri Salzman

In ancient Rome there lived a poor slave named Androcles. His cruel master made him work from daybreak until long past nightfall. Androcles had very little time to rest and very little to eat. One day, he decided to run away from his harsh master, even though he would be breaking the law.

In the dark of night, Androcles got up from the miserable heap of straw and rags that served as his bed. Crouching low so he was no taller than the bushes that dotted the fields, the young slave moved swiftly away from his master's land.

Clouds covered the moon that night, and Androcles crossed the open fields unseen. It was only when he came to the wild woods that Androcles dared to stand up tall again.

Androcles found a sheltered place at the foot of a tall tree. There he lay himself down on a bed of pine needles and fell fast asleep.

When Androcles awoke, he hiked deeper into the woods so he wouldn't be found by his master. There he looked for water and something to eat. But other than a few berries, there was no food to be found.

Day after day, Androcles searched for food. And day after day, he went hungry. Androcles grew so weary and weak that at last he was afraid he wouldn't live through the night. He had just enough strength to creep up to the mouth of a cave that he had passed many times. Androcles crawled into the cave and fell into a deep sleep.

As Androcles lay sleeping, a lion was hunting in the woods nearby. The lion liked to sleep in the daytime and hunt for his food at night.

The lion caught a small animal for his supper. He ate his meal beside a stream in the woods. Then he set off for his cave as the morning began to fill the sky with light.

Just before reaching the cave where Androcles slept, the lion stepped on the fallen branch of a thorn tree. A large thorn went deep into his paw.

The lion let out an angry roar, which woke Androcles with a terrible start. From the mouth of the cave, Androcles could see the lion rolling on the ground in pain. The lion's roars echoed loudly in the cave.

Androcles was terrified that the lion would attack him. But the lion held out his hurt paw to Androcles. Even from a distance, Androcles could see the large thorn in the lion's paw.

Androcles found some courage and came closer. He slowly sat down on the ground near the beast. To Androcles' astonishment, the huge lion flopped his great paw into the young man's lap.

Androcles spoke soothing words to the lion as he carefully pulled the thorn from the lion's paw. "Don't worry, handsome lion. We'll have this thorn out in no time," he said softly. The lion seemed to understand that Androcles was trying to help him. When the thorn was gone, the lion rubbed his head against Androcles' shoulder and purred a rumbling purr.

Androcles was no longer afraid of the lion. The lion was grateful to Androcles and didn't even mind that Androcles had moved into his cave.

The lion slept most of the day. And at night, he hunted for food while Androcles slept. In the morning, the lion would bring fresh meat to Androcles, who would build a little fire to cook his meal.

Every morning after Androcles ate, he and the lion played for a while in the woods nearby. The lion showed Androcles how much he liked him by rubbing his head against the young man and licking his hands and feet. Androcles scratched the lion behind the ears and petted his sleek back.

Androcles enjoyed his life with the lion very much. Thanks to the lion's successful hunting, Androcles was stronger and happier than he had ever been. When the lion lay down in the cave for his daytime sleep, Androcles would hunt for berries and nuts in the woods. It no longer mattered that he could not find enough berries and nuts for a man to live on.

One morning, as Androcles was cooking what the lion had brought him, five soldiers suddenly appeared and surprised him.

"We saw the smoke from your fire," they said. "We have come to arrest you for running away from your master."

Androcles tried to run from the soldiers, but they were too fast for him. Three soldiers sprinted after Androcles. When they caught him, they tied his hands behind his back.

The lion awoke with a start. Before he could even get to his feet, the other two soldiers threw a strong rope net over him, so he couldn't escape. They attached two ends of the net to a stout pole and carried the angry lion out of the woods.

Androcles, his hands bound behind him, was forced to march to Rome. He felt terrible that he had brought harm to his beloved friend, the lion. It was only when Androcles and the soldiers marched into Rome that he learned what was in store for himself.

The soldiers led Androcles toward a huge arena. One soldier said to Androcles, "You shall regret the day you ran away from your master! Your punishment is to fight a hungry lion!"

It was the custom in Rome at that time to entertain the people with battles. These battles were fought on the sandy floor of the arena, which was circled by rows and rows of seats.

The soldiers took Androcles to a prison under the arena seats. Then they left him alone in his prison cell.

A long time passed, but the soldiers did not return. From time to time Androcles heard the roar of hungry lions in another part of the arena.

At last Androcles heard a trumpet blast. Then he heard hundreds of feet shuffling overhead as people made their way to the seats in the arena.

Another blast sounded from the trumpet, and the bars to Androcles' prison were opened. A soldier roughly pulled Androcles out of his cell and pushed him onto the field. Then the prison bars went down again.

Androcles found himself in the middle of a huge arena. Hundreds of people were watching him. When a lion's roar sounded throughout the arena, the people grew excited. Poor Androcles felt sick with fear when he saw a lion in a cage at the far end of the arena. The trumpet sounded a third time, and the bars to the lion's cage were opened.

A lean lion bounded out of the cell, roaring with hunger. The crowd of people shouting in the arena sounded just like another mighty roar in Androcles' ears.

The lion crouched only for a moment, but in that moment Androcles recognized his friend from the forest. The lion let out another thundery roar and bounded across the arena in three long leaps. He stopped right in front of Androcles—and then gently lifted his big paw.

Androcles gave a mighty shout of joy. "Lion, you remember me!" he cried. He took the lion's paw in his hand and patted it lovingly. Then the lion rubbed his great head against the young man's shoulder.

The crowd of people in the arena was stunned into silence. They wondered why the hungry lion did not attack Androcles. The emperor motioned to Androcles.

"How did you tame this ferocious lion?" the emperor asked Androcles.

"I merely helped him when he needed help, Your Highness," Androcles replied. "That is why he spared my life."

The emperor freed Androcles and the lion. The lion returned to the wild woods, and Androcles became a free man in Rome.

Androcles often went for a walk in the woods to visit his good friend, who never forgot him.

The Five Brothers

Adapted by Brian Conway
Illustrated by Leanne Mebust

Once upon a time there were Five Brothers who all looked exactly alike. They lived with their dear mother in a little house beside the sea. The family kept to itself in that fine little house. They took good care of each other, and they never needed to go to the village nearby. For five very good reasons, they never needed anyone's help at all.

These Five Brothers looked just like each other, but they were not like everybody else. Their father had been a sorcerer once, and somehow these Five Brothers came to have special abilities. They could do things that no one else in the whole world could do.

The First Brother could slurp up the whole sea and hold it in his mouth. His skill was most useful when it came time for fishing.

The Second Brother could see through the back of his head. This was helpful for finding animals when the brothers went hunting in the woods.

The Third Brother could creep through even the smallest cracks. He was a great help to his mother when he crept through the walls and scared away the mice.

The Fourth Brother could stretch and stretch and stretch his legs. He could reach the finest fruit in the tallest trees.

The Fifth Brother could spin like a top, only faster. When he spun around, the Fifth Brother could spin into the ground just as deeply as needed to dig a fresh well.

When fishing day came, the First Brother, who could swallow the sea, set out with his brothers. He stood on the shore, leaned over, and slurped up the whole sea in his mouth. He could not hold the water very long, so his brothers hurried to gather the largest and finest fish for their mother.

Now it happened that, at that very moment, the king was having a swim in the sea just up the shore. The king liked complete privacy when he bathed. He had extremely large feet, you see, which he took great efforts to hide from the villagers.

With the water suddenly gone from the sea, however, the king's funny feet were laid bare for all the village to see.

"Who has taken the water away?" the king shouted to his guards. "Go and find him!"

Well, the Five Brothers gathered a few fish that morning until suddenly they heard angry cries coming from the village. Then they saw soldiers quickly approaching them. The First Brother tried to put the water back in its place just as quickly as he could, while his four brothers hurried home with their fish.

"Who do you think you are, taking all of the sea for yourself?" the king scolded. "You have made a fool of me, and you will be punished for it!"

The king decided the First Brother would be quickly banished from the kingdom. He ordered the guards to blindfold him, take him deep into the woods, and leave him there.

"Please, Your Highness," said the First Brother, "allow me to go and bid my dear mother good-bye."

"It is only fair," the king agreed.

The First Brother went home and asked the Second Brother to go back in his place.

The guards covered the Second Brother's eyes. They led him for many miles through the woods, twisting and turning away from any paths, around tree after tree.

Then they left him in the forest to fend for himself.

The Second Brother, who could see through the back of his head, knew exactly where he was, and how to get back. He came out of the woods even before the guards did. Walking home, though, he met the guards. They grabbed him and brought him before their king.

"You are clever," said the king, "but I know what to do with you."

The king ordered the guards to lock the Second Brother inside a box and carry him by buggy to another kingdom.

"Please, Your Highness," the Second Brother pleaded, "allow me to go and bid my dear mother good-bye."

"It is only fair," said the king.

The Second Brother went home and asked the Third Brother to go back in his place.

The Third Brother, who could creep through any crack, was locked in a box. Two soldiers lifted the box onto a buggy. They watched the buggy roll away down the road. They turned to go back to the castle and report the good news to the king, but standing right there behind them was the Third Brother! They grabbed him and brought him before their king.

"So you are more clever than I thought," growled the king. "I know what to do with you."

He ordered the guards to take the Third Brother out to sea, and drop him in the deepest waters.

"Please, Your Highness," the Third Brother pleaded, "allow me to go and bid my dear mother good-bye."

"It is only fair," said the king.

The Third Brother went home and asked the Fourth Brother to go back in his place.

The guards took the Fourth Brother aboard a boat. They sailed to the deepest waters and dropped him in. The Fourth Brother, who could stretch and stretch and stretch his legs, did just that until his feet could touch the bottom of the sea.

The guards stayed for most of a full day to watch him sink. The Fourth Brother did not sink. He happily stared back at them, his head bobbing up and down on the crest of the waves. Finally the guards pulled him out of the water and brought him before their king.

The king was very angry. "Take him to the dungeon and leave him there! He'll get no food or water!" the king shouted. "I never want to see him again!"

"Please, Your Highness," the Fourth Brother pleaded, "just let me go and bid my dear mother good-bye."

"I suppose it is only fair," said the king.

The Fourth Brother went home and asked the Fifth Brother to go back in his place.

The guards led the Fifth Brother to the cold, lonely dungeon of the king's castle. They threw him in among four hard stone walls and a solid stone floor.

"You'll get no food or water," the guards told him scornfully. "No one will ever see you again."

With that the guards slammed the thick stone door and sealed it shut.

Now the Fifth Brother, who could spin faster than a top, knew there was nothing below him but more solid rock. He could not dig, as he had done so many times for his mother.

"I shall spin in the other direction," the Fifth Brother decided. "Then I will go up."

The Fifth Brother turned and turned, spinning to a blur. He raised his arms from his sides and flew up, up, up through the roof above him.

The king was in his chamber, getting ready for bed, when the floor began to rumble.

Alarmed, the king jumped up on his bed as the Fifth Brother came spinning up through the floor!

"H-h-how did you...?" the angry king stuttered. "You are more than clever. You are a demon!"

He reached for his blade and called for his guards.

"Please, Your Highness," the Fifth Brother pleaded. "I am different, it is true. I have a gift, just like you."

"What do you mean?" the curious king asked.

"Your grand feet can be used for a very important job in the kingdom, Your Highness. Making mashed potatoes!" the Fifth Brother replied.

And so the king came to know that he, too, could do things that no one else in the whole world could do. He no longer felt foolish about his feet. He showed them off proudly each day as he walked barefoot through his kingdom.

Every day the king made enough mashed potatoes to feed the entire kingdom, and the Five Brothers shared their finest fish, meat, and fruit with all the king's subjects. Everyone in the kingdom had plenty, and many found they had gifts they never knew they had before. The Five Brothers and their mother became the most trusted and respected family in the land as they enjoyed a lifetime supply of mashed potatoes.

Icarus and Daedalus

Adapted by Sarah Toast
Illustrated by John Hanley

Long ago in ancient Greece there lived a very clever man named Daedalus. He was a great inventor and a skillful engineer and architect. Daedalus planned magnificent buildings that even had running water in the bathrooms. He was very proud of his skill.

Daedalus left Athens, the city of his birth, and went to the island of Crete in the blue Aegean Sea. He took with him his young son, Icarus.

King Minos of Crete commanded Daedalus to build a labyrinth, or maze, to imprison a fearful monster called the Minotaur. Daedalus built the huge labyrinth underneath the king's stone palace. The labyrinth had so many false turns and dead-ends that no one who entered it could ever find a way out.

CLASSIC CHILDREN'S STORIES

When the labyrinth was finished, the angry Minotaur was sealed inside it. When the Minotaur was hungry, his roar shook the palace. The king was satisfied.

Daedalus had been on Crete for a long time. He wanted to return home. So he went to King Minos and said, "Great King, with your permission, I shall take my leave. My work is done, and I wish to return to Athens with my son."

"You will do no such thing," said King Minos. "You know the secret of the labyrinth. How do I know you won't tell somebody how to find the way through the twisting passageways?"

"I pledge to you that I will do no such thing!" protested Daedalus.

But the king ordered his guards to seize Daedalus and Icarus. The father and son were locked in a tall tower at the very edge of the palace grounds.

Daedalus and Icarus were kept under close guard in the prison tower. It would have done them no good to escape the tower, because King Minos also ruled the surrounding seas. The king's soldiers inspected every ship that left the shores of Crete.

"Father, are we going to be locked in this tower forever?" asked Icarus.

"I am a great inventor, Icarus," replied Daedalus. "This is a difficult problem, but I shall think of a solution."

After days of being locked in the tower, Daedalus and Icarus needed fresh air. Daedalus climbed the stairway and led Icarus to the rooftop of the tower. Its great height made Daedalus fearful for Icarus' safety.

From the rooftop, Daedalus and Icarus watched the gulls and eagles soaring and gliding through the air. The birds flew very close to the tower.

"Icarus, my son, I have an idea," said Daedalus. "King Minos may rule the land and the sea, but he does not rule the air!"

"What do you mean?" asked Icarus. "Only birds can fly through the air."

"That is because they have wings!" said Daedalus. "I want you to help me catch some birds. We need many feathers of all sizes."

Daedalus watched closely the way birds use their wings to take off and fly. He studied the way feathers fit together to cover a bird's wing.

Icarus watched his father intently as he laid out a row of long feathers. Then his father laid a row of smaller feathers below that. He sewed them together with linen thread and a needle that he carried in his pouch.

Daedalus laid down many more rows of feathers which Icarus held in place for him. Finally, Daedalus softened some beeswax until it was sticky. With the wax, Daedalus fastened the rows of feathers together.

At last Daedalus was finished. When he held up the results of his work, Icarus saw that his father had made a beautiful pair of wings.

Daedalus tied the wings to his arms and shoulders with thin strips of leather. Cautiously, he fluttered the wings.

Daedalus then moved the great wings up and down with strong beats. He could feel himself lifting from the roof of the tower!

"Stop, Father! Make my wings now!" Icarus begged. Daedalus took his wings off and made a smaller set of wings for his son. Again he used wax to fasten many of the feathers. Then he tied the wings to Icarus.

"Just watch me first," said Daedalus to his son. "I'll try out the wings. If they work well, we'll both practice flying together."

Daedalus spread his wings, flapped them once, and caught the wind. Out he soared from the tower, lifting and falling on air currents.

Icarus thought his father looked like a god as he flew through the air. The boy couldn't wait any longer to fly himself.

Icarus stood on tiptoe at the edge of the tower, flapped his wings, and took off. As he swooped and soared, he shouted for joy. "I'm a bird! I'm a god!" he cried.

"Icarus! Go back!" shouted Daedalus. "Go back to the tower!"

Daedalus landed on the rooftop and called again to Icarus, "Come back!"

The boy circled around the tower twice and did a somersault in the air, before he came back to where his father stood anxiously on the rooftop.

"Son, we have much to learn about flying. And you have much to learn about obeying your father!" said Daedalus.

"We will have to practice many mornings to become strong and skillful enough to fly all the way across the Aegean," Daedalus explained to his son.

Daedalus and Icarus practiced flying every day. Their muscles became strong, and they increased their skill with their wings. When Daedalus judged that he and Icarus were ready to make the long trip over the sea, he sat Icarus down.

"Son, so far we have flown only over land near the tower. It is important that you heed my words. If you fly too low and too close to the waves," Daedalus explained, "your feathers will get damp. If that happens, your wings will be too heavy to keep you in the air."

"And if you fly too high," he went on, "the heat of the sun will melt the wax that holds your wings together."

"I understand, Father," said Icarus, but he was barely listening. He was so impatient to leap into the air again.

No sooner had his father finished telling Icarus not to fly too low or too high, than the boy ran to the very edge of the rooftop and leapt off. He flapped his outspread wings and headed for the sea with Daedalus close behind him.

Daedalus and Icarus were filled with delight at the wonder of flying. They flew higher and higher over woods and fields, heading for the sea. When the people down below looked up from their work, they were amazed to see what appeared like two gods flying gracefully overhead.

"Look!" Icarus shouted to his father. "Those people below really think we are gods flying this high."

"It doesn't matter, my son," Daedalus replied. "Just keep flying next to me. Don't stray too far."

When the two winged humans reached the blue Aegean, Daedalus shouted a reminder to his son to fly a middle course. Then away they flew together over the calm waters.

The father and son rode the rising currents of air like birds. They made long, slow turns, first one way and then the other in the brilliant blue sky. After a long time flying contentedly side by side, Daedalus flew past his son and took the lead.

Daedalus thought that if they kept flying with such grace and speed, they would be home soon, and then they could forget about being imprisoned on the island of Crete.

But Icarus was becoming reckless. He began diving and soaring behind his father.

Icarus did a somersault in the air and then caught up to where his father was. "We are like gods!" he shouted to his father. Daedalus looked back over his shoulder and smiled. He gestured for Icarus to stay behind him at a safe middle level.

Icarus, however, wanted to fly higher, up to the heavenly regions where the gods lived. While Daedalus flew on in front, unaware of his son's actions, Icarus beat his wings harder and rose up and up. The warmth of the sun felt good on his back, and Icarus rose still higher.

The same warm sun melted the wax on Icarus' wings. First only a few feathers and then many slipped off the wings as the wax turned to liquid in the sun's hot rays. Suddenly Icarus dropped straight down, down into the cold sea.

When Daedalus looked back, he could no longer see his son. Alarmed, Daedalus flew about in circles looking for the boy.

At last Daedalus flew close enough to the water to see feathers floating on the sea. He knew then that his beloved son had drowned.

Daedalus wept as he flew home, to the island of Sicily. If only his son had listened to him, then they would be flying to freedom together.

Daedalus lived alone on the island of Sicily, searching the skies for his beloved son who thought he could fly as high as the gods.

The Brownie of Blednock

Adapted by Jennifer Boudart
Illustrated by Gwen Connelly

Nighttime was falling over the town of Blednock. The people who lived there were doing what they did every ordinary day. Women stood on their doorsteps talking about the harvest. Children played in the town square. No one knew it, but something special was about to happen. It all began with a humming noise. The people of Blednock lined up along Main Street and looked down the road.

The humming kept getting louder. It was like the way you would hum to yourself if you were happy.

Somebody was coming down the road. People began to whisper to each other. Who was this visitor to Blednock? Visitors came from near and far, but no one had seen a person who looked like this before.

The stranger was as small as a boy, but he had a long, brown beard. He wore a long, pointed hat and tiny, curled-up shoes. He walked closer and closer, and the humming got louder and louder.

"Do you think he speaks our language?" whispered one man.

"Has he come to town to buy or sell?" wondered another.

Soon the crowd was quiet. That's when they heard what the stranger was humming: "Any work for Aiken-Drum? Any work for Aiken-Drum?"

What was an Aiken-Drum? No one seemed to know. The people were more curious than ever.

Then Granny, the wisest woman in the town, had something to say. "I think Aiken-Drum is what our visitor calls himself," she announced. "I believe he is a brownie." Granny hopped off the stump. She shook the brownie's hand. "Speak up, Brownie," said Granny. So he did.

The brownie had traveled far from his home. "The ways of brownies are very different from the ways of people," explained Aiken-Drum. "In our land, we learn to do good by serving others."

The little brownie explained there was not enough work in his land. "I don't need money, clothes, or fancy living," said the brownie. "I just need a dry place to sleep and something warm to drink at bedtime."

In return, Aiken-Drum promised to do any kind of work. All of the townspeople stared at each other, tongue-tied.

"I've heard brownies are the best workers," Granny told her neighbors. "If there's a town that needs a helping hand, it's Blednock," she added. Granny was right. The new church needed building. The bridge needed mending. All those jobs needed people to do them.

That is how a brownie came to live in Blednock. The blacksmith let Aiken-Drum sleep in a corner of his barn. Granny brought the brownie a warm drink at the end of each day.

The rest of the townspeople tried to spot Aiken-Drum whenever they could. He was always hurrying to one place or another. No one really saw him do any work. In fact, Aiken-Drum seemed to do all his work at night!

Every morning, the blacksmith found only an empty mug. Soon, all of the people of Blednock were sharing stories about the magical work of the little brownie.

"Aiken-Drum fixed a broken wheel on my wagon last night. He must have known that I was going to take my flour to the miller today," chuckled Baker Smith.

"While I was asleep with fever, Aiken-Drum came. He cleaned my whole house and cooked a big batch of soup!" crowed Old Mother Jones.

"Aiken-Drum brought all my sheep to safety. He took them into the barn just before last night's storm!" exclaimed Farmer Adams.

Wherever work needed to be done, Aiken-Drum was there. No one even had to ask. One evening as the mayor was leaving his office, he thought about asking the brownie to help him in the morning. But the very next morning, the work was already done. The only evidence of the little brownie was the empty mug he had left behind.

Since so much work was being done, the townspeople wondered if the brownie ever took breaks. And they worried that he wasn't getting enough rest for being so busy.

"He must be so tired," they said. "We must give him a vacation!"

"I don't need a vacation," Aiken-Drum said. "I take plenty of breaks when people aren't looking."

Aiken-Drum did take breaks from time to time. On still evenings, when fireflies began to wink, the brownie sat by the river. He would count the fireflies, skip stones across the water, and gaze at the stars in the sky. He used this time alone to clear his head and think about what kind of work came next.

But he was never alone for long. The children of Blednock usually came to join him by the river.

Children loved Aiken-Drum. He loved them, too. They crowded around, giggling and asking to play this game or that game:

"Tell us a story, Aiken-Drum."

"Teach us a song, Aiken-Drum."

"Show us a dance, Aiken-Drum."

"Play hide-and-seek, Aiken-Drum."

Aiken-Drum loved telling stories to the children. This was his favorite game to play. The children would gather around a fire that Aiken-Drum built for them. Then they would listen to the brownie's stories about goblins, fairies, dragons, and sorcerers. But their favorite stories were about other brownies just like Aiken-Drum.

Aiken-Drum would play with the children until their parents called them home for dinner. As they went off to their houses, Aiken-Drum went off to work.

Everyone thought things around Blednock were better than ever thanks to Aiken-Drum. Well, almost everyone. Miss Daisy Fain thought a little differently.

"I think things are unfair around Blednock," she said to people who would listen. "It is not right to make a brownie work so hard for nothing in return."

Miss Daisy's neighbors shook their heads at her. "Aiken-Drum made it plain, Miss Daisy," they would say with a sigh. "Brownies work only for the love of making people happy. Brownies do not need to be paid."

Miss Daisy just sniffed. She was sure he needed something more. He simply was too shy to ask. Finally, Miss Daisy decided to do what she knew was best. Everyone would thank her for it later, Aiken-Drum most of all.

One night, Miss Daisy tiptoed into the blacksmith's barn. The brownie was not there. Miss Daisy placed a pair of her husband's pants next to his mug. They would be too big for Aiken-Drum. They had plenty of patches and mud stains, too. Still, he would love them.

Well, you can guess what happened. Aiken-Drum took one look at those pants and knew what was happening. Someone had tried to pay him! His new friends had forgotten what mattered most to a brownie, so he disappeared that very night. No one saw him go.

The people of Blednock were very angry. Miss Daisy had tried to pay a brownie! Even worse, she had paid him with smelly, old pants!

After that, each day in Blednock was just like any other day. The people often spoke of Aiken-Drum with broken hearts and heavy sighs. The children were saddest of all. Still, once in a while when the wind was just right, they could hear the sound of humming floating across the river.

Brer Rabbit Outfoxes Brer Fox

Adapted by Megan Musgrave
Illustrated by Rusty Fletcher

I am going to tell you a story about Brer Rabbit and Brer Fox. But first, you ought to know a thing or two about rabbits and foxes.

Rabbits and foxes just never seem to get along. This is probably because foxes are always trying to make a meal out of rabbits, and rabbits are always trying to outfox those foxes.

Brer Rabbit was the craftiest rabbit ever to cross a fox's path. Brer Fox was always trying to catch Brer Rabbit, but Brer Rabbit always had a trick up his sleeve. One day, Brer Fox decided to get Brer Rabbit once and for all. "I'm a-gonna catch that hoppity rabbit and make me a fine meal outta him!" thought Brer Fox.

Brer Fox knew that Brer Rabbit liked to go over to the farmer's garden every day for carrots and cabbages. Brer Fox decided to hide behind a big tree on the road to the garden and wait for Brer Rabbit to pass. The tree was on the edge of a briar patch, full of bushes with thorns and burrs.

"I'm a-gonna wait right here for that sneaky rabbit an' cook 'im up in a rabbit stew!" said Brer Fox. He was very proud of his sneaky plan.

Soon Brer Rabbit came hippity-hopping down the road to the garden. Brer Fox jumped out from behind the tree and grabbed him up as quick as he could. "I'm a-gonna brew a stew out of you, Rabbit!" said Brer Fox.

Brer Rabbit had to do some fast talking. "You can cook me up in a big ol' pot an' serve me for dinner, but please don't throw me into dat briar patch yonder!" cried Brer Rabbit.

Brer Fox thought for a moment. "Now, maybe dat stew would be too much bother for me. I'm a-gonna roast you up instead!" he said.

"You can fire up your ol' stove an roast me an' serve me up with fried taters, but pleease don't throw me in dat briar patch!" pleaded Brer Rabbit.

This was starting to sound like a lot of work to Brer Fox. He really just wanted to get that rabbit out of his hair once and for all. "Naw, your scrawny hide ain't worth troublin' over. I'm jus' gonna string you up from that ol' hick'ry tree an' git you outta my hair," said Brer Fox.

"You kin string me up an' jus' let me swing, but whatever you do, pleeeaase don't throw me into that terr'ble briar patch!" cried Brer Rabbit.

Suddenly, Brer Fox knew just the thing to do. "Seems to me jus' about the worst thing I kin do is throw you into dat ol' briar patch, Rabbit," chuckled Brer Fox. "An' dat's jus' what I'm a-gonna do!" And with that, Brer Fox swung Brer Rabbit over his head and threw him into the middle of the briar patch.

"Yow! Oh, I'm a-gonna die!" yowled Brer Rabbit as he sailed through the air. But as soon as he landed in the briar patch, all Brer Fox could hear was Brer Rabbit hee-hawing and guffawing in gigglement. Brer Fox knew he'd been had again.

"Oh, Mister Fox, you shoulda known better! Y'see, I was born in dis here briar patch! I'm as happy as a crawfish in a river bed, an' now you're gonna have to find somebody else for dat dinner!" With that, Brer Rabbit bounced and bounded away through the briar patch.

Brer Fox was hoppin' mad. "I got to git dat rabbit good, once an' for all. He's a-goin' to Miss Goose's birthday party tomorrow, so I'm a-gonna make real friendly-like, an' go an' walk over to dat party with him. An' jus' when we git to crossin' over the river, I'm a-gonna throw dat rabbit in! He'll be gone for good, sure as shootin'!"

Brer Fox walked back to his house and stayed up all night planning his attack on Brer Rabbit.

The next day, Brer Rabbit was at his house getting all spruced up for Miss Goose's party. He combed up the hair on his ears, he brushed the cockleburs out of his tail, and he twisted his whiskers. He was about to put on his hat and start toward the door, when he heard a curious rustling in the leaves outside.

"Dat mus' be Brer Fox comin' to sneak up on me," Brer Rabbit said to himself. He tiptoed to the front window and peeked out of the curtain real easy-like.

When he saw Brer Fox come a-trottin' up his path, Brer Rabbit wrapped himself up in a blanket and acted real sick-like.

"What's all dis moanin' and a-groanin' about, Rabbit?" asked Brer Fox.

"Oh, I'm sick as an ol' dawg, Mister Fox. I ain't a-gonna make it to Miss Goose's party after all," sighed Brer Rabbit.

"C'mon, Brer Rabbit. Maybe you'll feel better soon," Brer Fox said.

"Oh no, Brer Fox! I'm too sick," Brer Rabbit said.

"This is a-gonna help wit' my plan jus' fine," thought Brer Fox.

He said to Brer Rabbit, "Now, you know yer gonna be sorry if you miss dat party, Rabbit. You come on wit' me, and I'm a-gonna carry you."

"You're mighty kind, Mister Fox. But surely I couldn't ride on your back without a saddle," said Brer Rabbit sneakily. Brer Fox didn't like the idea of putting on a saddle, but it went along nicely with his plan.

"I'd be glad ter put on a saddle," Brer Fox said, and he went off to find a saddle. While he was gone, Brer Rabbit picked a bunch of flowers for Miss Goose and hid them under the blanket. He fixed the blanket around his shoulders and then waited for Brer Fox to arrive.

Brer Fox soon came galloping back to Brer Rabbit's house wearing a saddle. "Up you go," said Brer Fox. "And take off dat blanket."

"I gotta wear dis blanket," said Brer Rabbit, as he shivered a little. "I can't afford ter catch cold."

"Have it yer way, Mister Rabbit, but ya better hurry or we'll be late for dat party," Brer Fox said.

"You're mighty kind, Mister Fox, but surely I couldn't ride along in dis saddle without havin' a bridle to steer you along," said Brer Rabbit.

So Brer Fox left again, this time to fetch a bridle.

While Brer Fox went to fetch a bridle, Brer Rabbit rummaged around in his closet until he found a brown paper bag. "I'm a-gonna give that fox a surprise he'll never forgit. He thinks he can outfox me, but I'm the foxiest rabbit this side of the Mississippi," Brer Rabbit said with chuckleness.

When Brer Fox returned, he was wearing a bridle as well as the saddle. He was all ready to go just like an old horse at the starting gate. "Rabbit," he said, "Miss Goose ain't a-gonna take it kindly if we're late for her party. You climb on up here now, an' let's git a-goin'." He chuckled to himself, thinking that soon he would be rid of that rabbit forever.

"You're terrible kind to an ol' sick rabbit like me, Mister Fox," said Brer Rabbit with a groan. He climbed into the saddle, and they were on their way.

As he was walking along, Brer Fox felt Brer Rabbit bustling around in the saddle. "What are you doin' back there, Rabbit?" he asked grumpily. He didn't like being Brer Rabbit's ride at all, but he figured this was the best way to get that rascal to the river.

"Oh, I'm fixin' up my blanket, Mister Fox. I got a chill somethin' terrible, you know," moaned Brer Rabbit. But really he was pulling out that brown paper bag.

After another minute, Brer Fox felt his rider shifting and shuffling around again. "What are you up to now, Rabbit?"

"Oh, Mister Fox, I'm just a-fixin' this ice bag on my poor ol' achin' head," groaned Brer Rabbit. But actually he was filling that brown paper bag with hot air. He knew Brer Fox had a plan up his sleeve, and he wasn't going to let him get away with any devilment.

Soon they came to the river. As Brer Fox stepped onto the wooden bridge that crossed over the water he thought, "I'm a-gonna throw that buggery rabbit off into kingdom come. Yep, this is just the spot."

But Brer Rabbit was ready for Brer Fox's sneaky trick. As soon as he felt Brer Fox stop over the middle of the river, he pulled his feet out from under the blanket. "What you stoppin' for, Mister Fox?"

"I'm a-gonna throw you into kingdom come, Rabbit!"

"Oh, no you're not. Giddyup!" shouted Brer Rabbit. And with that, he threw off his blanket and popped that bag right over Brer Fox's ears.

"Yeeoow!" shrieked Brer Fox. He thought a hunter had taken a clean shot at him. He jumped up in the air like a mad grasshopper and took off down the other side of the bridge.

Brer Fox galloped down the road toward Miss Goose's house with Brer Rabbit hanging on to the saddle and yodeling all the way.

"Giddyup, you ol' nag!" cried Brer Rabbit. Poor Brer Fox just kept on galloping along past the briar patch, past the farmer's garden, past the duck pond, and right up to Miss Goose's house. Miss Goose, Miss Sheep, and Miss Pig had heard Brer Rabbit yodeling from a long way off. When Brer Fox came galloping up with Brer Rabbit on his back, they thought they had never seen anything so funny.

"Brer Rabbit sure got Brer Fox's goat, all right!" clucked Miss Goose.

"Ol' Brer Fox won't want to go messin' with that rabbit agin, for sure!" bleated Miss Sheep.

"That Brer Rabbit is the trickiest critter this side of the Mississippi!" squealed Miss Pig.

"Whoa!" shouted Brer Rabbit as Brer Fox galloped up to Miss Goose's house. Brer Fox skidded to a stop and flopped on the ground right on the doorstep. "Aft'noon, ladies," said Brer Rabbit as he climbed down. "I am very sorry for bein' late, but my ol' horse here jus' don't run like he used to." Miss Goose, Miss Sheep, and Miss Pig nearly burst with gigglement.

Poor old Brer Fox sat in the front yard, sputtering and gluttering and catching his breath. He was so mad he could spit. "That rabbit tricked me good dis time. I don' know how I'm a-gonna do it, but I'm a-gonna git dat rabbit one day, once an' for all," he fumed. Brer Fox felt a little bit better after tasting Miss Goose's birthday cake.

Ever since that day, sly ol' Brer Fox has kept trying to outsmart Brer Rabbit. And ever since that day sneaky Brer Rabbit has been just one step ahead of Brer Fox. So if you ever see a rabbit hopping around in a briar patch, or if you glimpse a fox snooping around a farmer's garden, it just might be ol' Brer Rabbit and Brer Fox trying to outfox each other again.

Ali Baba

Adapted by Brian Conway
Illustrated by Anthony Lewis

In a town in Persia there lived a man called Ali Baba. He was a poor woodcutter, and he struggled greatly each day to feed his wife and children. All he ever wanted was to own a shop in the town, sell goods to his neighbors, and have plenty for his family.

One day Ali Baba was cutting wood in the forest. He saw a troop of men on horseback approaching. Ali Baba thought these men were robbers, so he climbed a tree to hide.

Ali Baba counted 40 men. He wondered whether this could be the band of Forty Thieves he had heard so much about, the robbers that all of Persia feared. Their leader dismounted and stepped around a bush toward a large rock wall. The powerful man faced the wall, and Ali Baba clearly heard him shout, "Open, sesame!"

A door opened in the rock wall, revealing a secret opening to a cave. The leader stepped in, and the other robbers followed him.

Ali Baba waited until the thieves filed out from the cave. Their Captain closed the door, saying, "Shut, sesame!" Then the thieves rode away.

When he was sure they were gone, Ali Baba stepped toward the rock, as the Captain had done. Then he shouted, "Open, sesame!" And the door opened for him just as miraculously as it had for the Captain of Thieves.

Ali Baba stepped through the threshold to find a large room, filled at every inch with all sorts of valuables, so brilliant with gold, silver, and jewels that Ali Baba had to squint.

He feared the robbers might soon return. He hurriedly made a pouch with his cloak and gathered as much gold as he could carry. Ali Baba remembered in his haste to say, "Shut, sesame!" when he left the cave.

Ali Baba did not notice one small but important thing as he hurried away from the cave to share his fortune with his family. A single gold coin dropped from his cloak to the base of the bush that covered the secret door. Fortunately for Ali Baba, the thieves did not notice the coin that day, or the next day either, or for several days until a few weeks later.

The Captain of Thieves caught sight of the single coin's glimmer one day. He was very angry.

"How could you drop this and risk revealing our hiding place!?!" the Captain shouted at his 39 robbers.

"But, Master," the thieves told him meekly, "we know the punishment for such mistakes is most severe. Surely none of us has done this."

"Then we have been found out," the Captain growled. He paced for several minutes. Then he announced, "We must learn who is newly rich in the town. That man and all his family must die."

By now Ali Baba had opened the shop of which he'd always dreamed. He was a fair and generous shop owner. After all, he could afford it, with a pile of gold at home and more in the secret cave whenever he would need it. He was happy, his family had plenty, and every neighbor was his friend.

Ali Baba hired a helper named Morgiana. She was a very clever and beautiful young lady. She enjoyed her work at the shop. And Morgiana cared for Ali Baba and his family very much.

Then a stranger came calling at the shop one day. He asked Morgiana many questions about the owner, Ali Baba. The stranger's questions worried Morgiana. She vowed to keep a watchful eye on the shop.

The thief in disguise returned to the robbers' cave. "His name is Ali Baba, Captain," said the thief. "He lives behind his new shop in town. He was a poor woodcutter only a few weeks ago."

"Go back there at nightfall," the Captain ordered. "Mark the house with this white chalk, and later, I will take twenty men there and finish him."

As he was told, the thief crept in the shadows to mark Ali Baba's home. Little did he know that clever Morgiana had spotted him. She followed with white chalk, too, and marked all the shops.

When the Captain and his 20 thieves arrived later that night, they found every shop was marked. They did not know which shop to attack, so they crept away in shame.

Their leader was very angry. "Will somebody get this right, once and for all?" cried the Captain.

One brave thief stepped forward. "Here is some red chalk," the Captain offered. "Mark the shop again, and I will lead 30 men to storm Ali Baba's home and end this threat."

The thief did as he was told, but again Morgiana played her trick on the Captain and his 30 thieves.

The Captain decided to use all his power against Ali Baba. The Forty Thieves gathered together and made a plan. The Captain would disguise himself as an oil merchant. He would lead a train of mules that carried 39 barrels. The thieves would hide inside the barrels and await their Captain's signal. It seemed like an excellent plan.

Early that night, they arrived at Ali Baba's shop.

"I have brought some oil to sell at market tomorrow," the Captain lied. "But tonight I need a place to stay. Will you take me in?"

Ali Baba was as generous as usual. "Of course you can stay here," he replied. "Leave your cargo in back. There is hay there for the mules. Then come in for dinner."

In the yard, the Captain whispered to his men, "Wait until you hear my signal. Then you must leave your barrels and storm the house."

Morgiana helped Ali Baba's family feed their guest. She thought it strange that a man would arrive so early for market, but the oil merchant seemed very polite.

After everyone had gone to bed, Morgiana finished cleaning up. Her lamp ran out of oil. She thought she'd have to finish cleaning in the dark until she remembered the many barrels of oil in the yard.

She walked up to the first barrel. A voice came through and whispered, "Is it time?"

Morgiana sensed danger. She answered, "Not yet, but soon." Then, gathering some hay around each barrel, Morgiana lit the hay with a torch. The 39 cowardly thieves coughed from the smoke. They popped out from their barrels and ran away to keep from getting burned.

Morgiana watched the men run off into the distance. She waited until all of them had gone, then she took some water from the house to put out the flames.

Just then, the Captain of Thieves said good-bye to Ali Baba and left through the back door where the barrels were burning.

The Captain of Thieves made his signal, but none of his men moved. He smelled the smoke then and realized something had gone wrong again. He was not surprised. He decided that he couldn't trust his men ever again. The Captain looked around the town for the thieves, but they were nowhere to be found.

The Captain quickly returned to the cave to look for his 39 robbers there. But the robbers were certain they'd be punished for running off, and each one vowed the Captain would never see him again.

The Captain was all alone now. He was the only thief left to protect the treasure in the cave. On his own, the single thief decided he would have to use all his cunning and energy to plan his revenge. It would take time, too, he knew.

The Captain began drawing up his plans on the sandy floor of the cave. It took him a month to perfect his plan, but he was soon ready to carry it off. This time, he vowed, it would work.

The Captain dressed carefully as a shop owner, went into town, and took up lodgings at an inn. He opened a shop across the road from Ali Baba's shop. Every day he watched Ali Baba come and go from his shop across the street. The Captain studied Ali Baba's habits and wrote them down in a book. "This information will be very helpful to my plan," said the Captain. "Soon, I will know enough about Ali Baba to destroy him and his family."

"The buildings are so tall that you can't see the tops of them," Alistair He waited in his disguise for precisely the right moment. Then he knew it would be time to see Ali Baba.

Ali Baba wanted to invite the newest shop owner over for dinner. He sent his son across the road with several gifts of friendship. Cogia Hassan graciously accepted the gifts but refused the invitation on many occasions. It wasn't the right time, yet.

After a full year had passed, the Captain at last agreed to dine with Ali Baba. He brought a basket of fine goods. He smiled as he met Ali Baba and his family, but he secretly carried a dagger in his cloak. The blade was intended for Ali Baba and his son.

Morgiana quickly served Cogia Hassan as Ali Baba and his son spoke with their new guest.

Morgiana saw the dagger first. She thought Cogia Hassan had looked familiar, and now she knew why. He was the devious oil merchant who had threatened Ali Baba's household one long year ago.

Morgiana wished to save her beloved benefactors. She wore a headdress and several long, flowing silk scarves. She called for a servant to play music, then entered the dining room to dance for their guest.

Morgiana danced close to Cogia Hassan. She brushed him with a silk scarf. Stepping behind Cogia Hassan, Morgiana wrapped the scarf lightly around his arms then pulled hard. He could not move.

"What are you doing?" Ali Baba cried. "This man is our guest."

"This man is your enemy," she explained. "Would a friend bring a dagger to dinner? This man is the Captain of the Forty Thieves!"

At that, Ali Baba's son seized the dagger, and the Captain of Thieves was sent directly to prison.

"I owe you my life, Morgiana," Ali Baba said. "Please marry my son and join our family in name as well as deed."

Morgiana agreed. They celebrated a splendid wedding. Ali Baba told his son and Morgiana about the riches in the secret cave and the words that would open the door. All their children and their grandchildren were rich forevermore.

Rip Van Winkle

Adapted by Pegeen Hopkins
Illustrated by John Lund

I f the legends of old are true, there is a touch of magic in the Catskill Mountains. They are the tall and beautiful cliffs that rise up far from the Hudson River. They reach so high that they nearly scrape the sky. If you look real close, on a clear day, you can see trails of smoke rising. The smoke comes from a sleepy, little town sitting at the base of the mysterious hills. This village was first settled by Dutchmen, in the oldest times, when the country was still very young. Many years ago, a simple, friendly man lived in that very town. His name was Rip Van Winkle.

Rip was a kind neighbor, loved by nearly everyone in town. When he walked through the streets, packs of children followed in his steps. They would ask for piggyback rides. Rip always agreed. He played games with them too, flew kites and shot marbles with them. Even the neighborhood dogs loved him. They never barked when Rip passed by.

Rip Van Winkle's only fault was that he hated work. It is not that he avoided any kind of moving around. He liked to go fishing in a stream. He would walk for hours hunting squirrels with his dog, Wolf. And Rip would never turn down a neighbor who asked for help.

But at home, Rip Van Winkle could do nothing right. His fences were always falling down. Weeds grew faster in his yard than anywhere else. And if his cow wasn't running away, she was ruining the fields.

His children were just as raggedy as his farm. They ran around wild, in ripped clothes. His son, Rip, was worst of all. "That young Rip," everyone said, "is going to turn out just like his father."

One autumn afternoon, Rip and Wolf wandered to the top of one of the highest mountains, by mistake. Late in the day, Rip threw himself down on the ground and enjoyed the beautiful countryside.

Just when Rip prepared to pick himself up and start home, he heard someone call his name. He turned and saw no one. Then he started down the hill. "Rip Van Winkle," he heard once more. Wolf began to growl. The fur on the back of his neck stood on end.

Rip looked around again. This time, his eyes fell on a strange little man, climbing up the hill. On his shoulder, the man carried a huge barrel almost bigger than himself.

"Would you help me with this?" the little man asked.

"Of course," Rip replied. The man made Rip nervous, but he would never say no when asked for help.

Rip and the man walked up a small hill, while Wolf followed. As they made their way up, Rip heard loud claps and crashes. It sounded just like thunder. It seemed to come from the direction they were headed. Rip checked the sky. It still looked clear and blue. "There must be a thunder shower on the other side of the mountain," Rip guessed. Sudden rain showers were common this high in the mountains.

Passing through a deep crack in the mountain, they entered into a round clearing of grass. Mountains rose up on all sides. Once inside, Rip saw something very strange. On a flat spot in the center, there stood a crowd of little men. What a strange group they were.

What these men were doing was even more strange. Rip rubbed his eyes. The little men were bowling! They were throwing a ball at nine wooden pins that were sitting on the grass. No one made a noise. But every time the tiny ball rolled along the ground, the sound of thunder broke out.

When Rip and the little man reached the group, the men turned and stared at him.

One tiny man took the barrel from Rip's hand. He poured a thick, dark liquid from it into small mugs. Rip's companions motioned for him to take a mug for himself. Rip did. And he drank more than one glass.

Once Rip had finished several glasses, he felt tired. His eyes drooped, his vision blurred, and he drifted off into a deep sleep.

When Rip finally opened his eyes, it was morning. The sun shone high in the sky. Rip was lying with his head resting on a tree, right where he'd been when he first met the little man.

"Have I been asleep here all night?" Rip exclaimed in a panic. "Mrs. Van Winkle is going to be so angry! What am I going to tell her?"

Rip whistled for Wolf. The dog did not come running. "Maybe that little man ran off with my dog," Rip said. "Or maybe Wolf went home. I had better get there, too."

As he stood up, Rip's knees cracked. His legs hurt, as if he had not used them in a while. "Sleeping outside can't be good for me," Rip thought. His stomach growled. He was hungry for breakfast. When Rip started off down the hill, he was sad and a little confused.

As Rip got close to his village, he ran into a number of people. He did not know any of them. They were dressed strangely, too. He looked at them in surprise and saw looks of surprise on their faces as well.

Finally, Rip looked down to see what everyone was staring at. A long beard flowed down to his belly!

In town, a group of children raced after Rip, yelling and hollering. None of them looked familiar. Their dogs ran after him, barking and biting at Rip's heels. They did not know him, and he did not know them. Even the town itself looked different.

Rip passed streets full of houses that were not there before. His favorite places to visit were gone. Strange names appeared above the doors. He saw faces he did not know looking out at him from the windows.

Rip began to worry. He wondered if he and the entire town had fallen under some horrible spell. This had to be his hometown, the one he had left just the afternoon before. He looked over his shoulder. There, he saw the Catskill Mountains, the same as they had always been.

"I better head home," Rip said. "Things will surely be all right once I see Mrs. Van Winkle and the children."

After lots of searching and scratching his head, Rip was able to find his farm and his farmhouse. The house didn't look at all like he remembered it looking. The fence had fallen down completely, and the roof had partly fallen in. And there wasn't a soul in sight. Rip looked around the farm for some kind of movement.

Rip walked up to the house slowly. With each step Rip became more and more afraid. The front door was swinging in the breeze.

Rip stepped inside the house. It was dark, and dust covered every inch of the space. No one had lived in the house for many years it seemed.

Rip ran to the center of town, looking for something familiar. His friends at the inn would have to know him. The building was gone though. In its place stood a tall pole topped with a red and white striped cloth waving in the wind. Then a group of men walked up to Rip.

"What are you doing here?" a tall man asked Rip. "Are you a Federalist or a Democrat? Did you fight in the Revolution?"

Rip had no idea what the man was talking about. Rip asked them, "Does anybody here know Rip Van Winkle?"

"Oh, sure," several of them answered. "That's Rip Van Winkle there, standing against that tree." Rip followed their pointed fingers. He saw someone that looked exactly like his old lazy self. The tall man walked up to Rip. He looked him in the eye and asked, "And just who exactly are you?"

"I was myself last night," Rip said. "I fell asleep on the mountain. Now everything has changed."

Right then a young woman with a baby in her arms pushed her way out of the crowd. She wanted to get a look at this old, gray-bearded man.

The young woman walked up to Rip. The chubby baby took one look at Rip and became afraid. He started to cry.

"This man won't hurt you," said the woman to the crying baby. Her voice and manner seemed so familiar to Rip.

"What is your name, Miss?" Rip asked gently.

"Judith Gardenier," she replied.

"And your father's name?" Rip asked.

"Oh, the poor man. Rip Van Winkle was his name. It's been twenty years since he took off into the mountains. His dog came home, but my father never returned. We have heard nothing about him since then. I was just a little girl then," the woman answered.

Rip had just one question left to ask. He posed the question with a trembling voice, "And what about your mother?"

"She just recently died," the woman answered.

Hearing this, Rip could no longer contain himself. "I am your father," he cried as he hugged her. "Once I was young Rip Van Winkle. Now I am old Rip Van Winkle. Doesn't anyone here know me?"

An old woman walked right up to Rip in the center of the crowd. She put her face almost to his, so she could see clearly. "Sure enough," she said. "Welcome home, Rip Van Winkle. Where have you been all these years?"

It did not take Rip long to tell his story. For him it had passed in one night. Some of the townspeople believed him. They listened with wide eyes and amazement. Others shook their heads. They thought he was crazy.

Judith asked her father to come live with her and her husband. Rip settled in quickly at his daughter's comfortable house. As for Rip Junior, he turned out to be just as lazy as his father had been.

At first Rip was quite sad. He had been away so long, and he missed so much. Then Rip swore that he would make each day special, because he had spent so many of his days asleep.

Rip soon returned to his favorite places. He could always be found on the bench in front of the inn. Every time a stranger approached the inn door, Rip would tell his strange story.

Some folks didn't believe Rip's tale of little men and years of sleeping. But he kept repeating it. He wanted people to know how important it is to make every day special.

All of the old Dutchmen believed him, though. They crowded around him every day to hear new bits of his incredible story.

To this day, whenever thunder crackles in the Catskills, the old Dutchmen say it is the gnomes playing their strange lawn game. Who knows, it just may be true.

The Twelve Dancing Princesses

Adapted by Sarah Toast
Illustrated by Pamela R. Levy

Long ago there lived a king who had twelve beautiful and clever daughters. The princesses all slept in the same huge room, with their twelve pretty beds in a row.

The king loved his daughters dearly, but he was becoming concerned about what they did each night. Even though the king carefully locked the door of the princesses' room every night, the next morning he found the princesses tired and out of sorts. More puzzling still, their tiny silk dancing slippers were worn to shreds.

Every day, the king ordered twelve new pairs of beautiful silk shoes for his daughters. Every night he locked them in their great room, only to find a row of worn-out shoes.

The next morning, the king begged his beloved daughters to explain why they were so tired and pale, and why their dancing shoes were in shreds. But the princesses merely murmured, "Beloved Papa, we have been sleeping peacefully in our beds all night."

The king thought of a way to find out the truth. At once, he issued a proclamation declaring that the first man to solve the mystery of where the twelve princesses went to dance every night would choose a wife from among them. Then the couple would rule the kingdom together after the king's death. The king warned, however, that anyone who tried to discover the princesses' secret had only three days and three nights to succeed. After that, the suitor would be banished from the kingdom forever.

It was not long before a prince arrived at the palace to try his luck. The king made the young prince feel welcome.

When evening came, the prince was led to a small chamber next to the great room shared by the twelve princesses. The door between the two rooms was left open. The princesses could not leave their room without being seen by the prince.

When the princesses filed into their room that night, the prince was enchanted by their beauty. He gladly accepted the cup of wine offered to him by the eldest princess. In no time, he was sound asleep in his bed.

When the prince awoke the next morning, the princesses were asleep in their beds. The prince was dismayed to see twelve pairs of worn-out shoes!

The next night and the night after that, the same thing happened. The king banished the prince from the kingdom.

Many other princes met the same fate. The king began to despair of ever finding out where his daughters danced at night.

Then one day a poor soldier came limping along the road. He had been wounded and could no longer serve in battle. The soldier had no sooner sat down by the side of the road to eat some bread and cheese when an old woman appeared all dressed in rags.

"Won't you have a bite to eat with me?" said the kind soldier to the woman. He offered her half of his simple meal.

"Where are you going?" asked the woman.

"I am going to the city to find work," replied the soldier. When he saw the sad look on the old woman's face, the soldier joked, "Don't worry about me! Perhaps I can find out how the princesses wear out their shoes!"

The old woman surprised the soldier by saying, "Heed my words! Do not drink the wine that the princesses offer you. Pretend to fall asleep. And take this cloak, which will make you invisible. You can follow the princesses and discover their secret!"

The soldier didn't know what to think. He thanked the old woman politely and continued on his way. When the chill wind blew, the soldier put on the cloak and discovered that it did indeed make him invisible. He headed at once to the king's palace, where he was made welcome.

In the evening, the soldier was led to the little room next to the princesses' great room. Soon the eldest princess brought the soldier a cup of wine. He pretended to drink the sweet wine, letting it trickle down under his chin and onto his ragged scarf. Then he climbed into bed and pretended to fall asleep.

When the eldest princess heard the soldier's snores, she quietly said to her sisters, "He is as foolish as the others. Make haste. We must get ready for the ball!"

The twelve princesses chattered and laughed as they dressed in their best ball gowns and jewels and arranged each other's hair. Only the youngest princess felt uneasy. "Something just doesn't feel right tonight," she said.

"Don't be such a little goose," said the eldest princess fondly. "That soldier is sound asleep. He won't wake up until morning!"

When the twelve princesses were ready, they put on their new dancing shoes. Then the eldest princess tapped on her bedpost three times. The bed descended into the floor and became a long flight of stairs.

The eldest princess stepped down into the opening in the floor. One by one, her sisters followed her.

The soldier saw the princesses walk down the stairs. He sprang out of bed and threw on the cloak. Then he followed the youngest princess down the stairway.

Because his leg was lame, the soldier stumbled and stepped on the hem of the youngest princess' gown. She shrieked with alarm, "Someone has stepped on my gown!"

"Don't be so skittish," said the eldest princess. "Your dress must have caught on a nail."

The princesses and the soldier continued down many flights of stairs and along many corridors until at last they came to a passageway bordered by marvelous silver trees. As the princesses hurried through, the soldier reached up and broke off a glittery, shiny branch of silver leaves. When the branch cracked, the youngest princess cried out again. "Did you hear that? I think someone is following us."

"Don't worry, dear," said the eldest princess. "That was just a welcoming salute from the princes who await us."

Next they came to a gleaming forest of golden trees, and then into a garden where the trees grew sparkling diamonds.

The soldier broke off some golden branches and a spray of diamonds so he would have a way to prove his story to the king. Each time he did so, the youngest princess cried out.

"There it is again! Someone or something is following us. I just know it," said the youngest princess.

"You must be imagining it," replied the oldest princess. "Now hurry along or we'll be late."

The twelve princesses hurried down a broad avenue of diamond trees to the edge of a beautiful lake. There, twelve princes awaited them in twelve little painted boats. Each princess took the hand of a handsome prince and joined him in a boat.

The soldier just had time to hop in the boat with the youngest princess and her companion. The prince struggled as they moved across the lake.

"I don't know why," said the prince, "but it is much more difficult to row my boat than it was last night!"

The youngest princess became suspicious again.

On the other side of the lake stood a splendid castle. Every window was glowing with light, and fireworks lit up the sky. As the beautiful little boats approached the castle, a fanfare of trumpets announced the arrival of the twelve dancing princesses.

The princes helped the princesses out of the small boats and led them to the castle.

Again, the youngest princess heard a rustling next to her. She knew her sisters would not believe her, so she kept quiet this time. But she kept listening for more movement in the grass.

The princes and princesses stepped into the castle, where beautiful music welcomed them into the ballroom. They had a large feast where the most delicious food was served. The soldier made sure no one was watching as he swiped an apple off the long banquet table. The youngest princess did notice, however, that someone had taken a small sip from her cup sitting on the table. She still couldn't explain her suspicions, so she remained quiet about them.

After dinner, the princesses danced with their princes for half the night. They turned and stepped across the floor as the princes led the way. The soldier joined the dancing unseen and unnoticed. He watched the couples twirl across the ballroom floor.

After many hours, the youngest princess became very tired. She left the dancing and sat down at the banquet table. She was about to drink from her cup when she noticed that it was empty. "I know this cup was full when I left the table," thought the youngest princess.

"Someone has tasted my drink!" she exclaimed.

"Nonsense, little sister. Come back and enjoy the dancing!" said her older sisters in reply. "The night is almost over!"

Soon the princesses' slippers were worn out.

The princes rowed the twelve princesses back across the lake, and this time the soldier rode with the eldest sister. The princesses bade their princes good-bye and promised to return the next night.

Then the princesses hurried back the way they had come, through the garden of diamonds and the forests of gold and of silver. They retraced their steps through the corridors and up the staircases.

The princesses were so tired that they slowed down at the top of the last set of stairs. The soldier was able to dash ahead of them, throw off his cloak, and jump into his bed.

The princesses dragged themselves into their room and put their worn and tattered shoes in a row. The eldest princess checked on the soldier to be sure he was asleep and said to her sisters, "We are safe!" With that, all twelve sisters fell fast asleep.

The soldier wanted to see the forests and the castle again, so he followed the princesses the next night and the next. The third night, the soldier took a golden cup from the castle to show the king.

The next morning the king sent for the soldier and asked him, "Good soldier, have you discovered where my daughters dance their shoes to shreds every night?"

"Your Highness, I have," said the soldier. "They go down a hidden staircase. Then they walk through three enchanted forests to a beautiful lake. Twelve princes take them across the lake to a castle where they dance the night away."

The king couldn't believe the soldier's story until the soldier showed him the golden cup and the branches of silver, gold, and diamonds. Then the king summoned his daughters, who at last admitted the truth. The eldest princess laughed and said, "I didn't think it could be done, but the soldier certainly has outwitted us!"

The king told the soldier that he could choose one of the princesses to be his wife. It didn't take the soldier very long to make his decision. He had already decided that he liked the eldest princess best. She was clever and spirited as well as beautiful. For her part, the princess thought the soldier was clever and kind.

The soldier was given royal chambers and royal garments to wear. He and the eldest princess were married, and the wedding guests happily danced the night away.

The City Mouse and the Country Mouse

Adapted by Lisa Harkrader
Illustrated by Dominic Catalano

Once upon a time a country mouse named Oliver lived in a hole under the root of a big old oak tree. Oliver loved the sound of squirrels chattering during the day and crickets chirping at night. He loved the smell of rich dirt and hearty grass all around him.

One day Oliver invited his city cousin, Alistair, for a visit. Before Alistair arrived, Oliver tidied up his hole. He straightened his oak leaf bed. He spread fresh pine needles on the floor. He scrubbed the tuna can he used for a table and polished the bottle caps he used as plates.

Then Oliver sat by the entrance to his hole, gazed out at the stars, and waited for his cousin Alistair to arrive.

When Alistair arrived, he set his fine leather suitcase on the rug of pine needles. "I say, cousin, is this your cellar?" he asked Oliver.

"No," said Oliver, "it's my home."

Oliver showed Alistair the back of the hole, where he stored his grain. He led Alistair up onto the nob of the old oak root, where he sometimes sat to watch the sunset. Then he sat Alistair down at the tuna can table and served him a late dinner of barleycorn and wheat germ.

Alistair nibbled his meal politely. "This certainly tastes as though it's good for me." He coughed and swallowed. "A bit dry, perhaps. Could I bother you for a cup of tea?"

Oliver brewed up a thimble of dandelion tea. When the thimble was empty, Oliver changed into his long johns, Alistair changed into his silk pajamas, and the mice settled into their oak leaves for the night.

Oliver awoke early the next morning, as usual. A robin family twittered in the old oak tree. A rooster crowed at a nearby farm.

Alistair squeezed his pillow over his ears. "What is that confounded racket?" he mumbled.

"That's the sound of morning in the country," said Oliver. "It's the wonderful music that makes me want to leap from my bed each morning and start the new day."

Alistair pulled the pillow from his face and opened one eye. "You start your day in the morning?" he asked. "Good heavens, cousin, I usually don't rise till noon."

"Here in the country we rise at dawn," Oliver replied as he buttoned his overalls. Then he pulled on his work boots and pushed his wheelbarrow out into the morning sun.

Alistair rolled to the edge of his oak leaf bed. He slid his feet into his shiny black dress shoes and followed his cousin outside.

Oliver gathered acorns and stacked them near his hole.

Alistair yawned and leaned against the root of the old oak tree.

Oliver shucked the seeds from the tall rye grass and carried them to the back of his hole where they would stay dry.

Alistair wiped the dust from his shoes with his silk handkerchief.

Oliver ventured into a nearby field to find fallen cornstalks. He dragged the stalks home and peeled off the husks. He rubbed the kernels of corn loose and piled them neatly against the root of the old oak.

"There." Oliver rubbed his hands on his overalls. "That's done."

"Thank goodness." Alistair collapsed into the wheelbarrow. "Now that we've finished the work, I'd say it's time for a bit of a snack and a nap. Wouldn't you?"

Oliver giggled at Alistair. "The work isn't finished," Oliver said. "We still have to carry in water and hack out that root that is growing down into my kitchen. And winter is coming, don't forget. Time to gather up rags and bits of grass to keep the snow out and the hole snug and warm."

Alistair sighed. "I'm simply not cut out for the country life," he said. "You work too hard for your dinner. And all you end up with is a pile of birdseed. A mouse could starve to death here. Come home with me for a while. I'll show you the good life."

"But I have so much work to do here," Oliver said.

"Exactly!" Alistair replied. "That is why you need to come with me and take a vacation from country life. Come to the city."

Oliver finally agreed to follow his cousin to the city.

Alistair packed his silk pajamas into his fine leather suitcase. Oliver packed his long johns into his beat-up carpet bag. The two mice set out for Alistair's home in the city.

Oliver followed Alistair over fields and valleys. As they walked, Alistair told Oliver about all of the things they would see soon.

"The buildings are so tall that you can't see the tops of them," Alistair said. "Some of the buildings are taller than the clouds. And there are people everywhere!"

Oliver kept following his cousin into subway tunnels and down crowded city sidewalks.

"The cars are very big, and they go very fast. Have you ever ridden in a car, Oliver?" Alistair asked.

"What is a car?" asked Oliver.

Alistair giggled and said, "You'll find out soon enough."

The cousins crossed busy streets until they finally reached the luxury hotel where Alistair lived.

Alistair stopped in front of the door and held his arms up. "Polished marble floors and shiny brass knobs," he said. "This is how mice are supposed to live."

Oliver stared up at the revolving glass door. "H-h-how do we get inside, Alistair?" he asked.

"Wait till the opening comes around, then run through," Alistair replied. The door swung around, and Alistair disappeared inside.

Oliver took a deep breath. He saw an opening and dove inside. He tried to run through, like Alistair had said, but his carpet bag was caught on the edge of the door.

"Whoa!" Oliver cried as he went round and round. He spun so many times, he couldn't tell whether he was right side up or upside-down.

Oliver whirled and whirled, and he might still be whirling to this very day if Alistair hadn't leaped up, tugged the bag free, and dragged Oliver inside the hotel.

Oliver sat on the marble floor to catch his breath. Then he followed Alistair across the lobby and through a small crack in the wall hidden by velvet draperies.

"My apartment," Alistair said when they were inside.

Oliver looked around in amazement. Alistair's home was filled with golden candlesticks, fine china, and linen napkins embroidered with the hotel's name.

"We're under the bandstand," Alistair said and pointed out the hole that was his front door. "An orchestra plays out there, and ladies and gentlemen dance every night until dawn."

"How can you sleep with all the noise?" asked Oliver.

"Sleep?" said Alistair. "I can sleep during the day. We do things a little differently here. Dinner, for example. At a five-star hotel, dinner begins with hors d'oeuvres."

Oliver followed his cousin out the door.

"Would you like pasta or tuna or cheese?" Alistair asked, but Oliver had never heard of any of these.

Alistair led Oliver through the dining room. They hid behind potted plants and raced under tablecloths. They waited until the chef went to check something in the dining room, then scampered across the kitchen and into the pantry.

The pantry was dark. Oliver stumbled. Something skidded across the pantry and thwack!

"Do be careful," said Alistair. He opened the pantry door a crack.

In the dim light Oliver could see what he'd stumbled over. "It's a-a-a . . ."

"A mousetrap." Alistair scooted it under a shelf with his paw. "You'll learn to stay away from them."

Alistair led Oliver up the shelves to the hors d'oeuvres. Alistair gobbled fancy crackers, nibbled pasta, and even managed to chew a hole in a tin of smoked salmon.

"Now this," said Alistair, patting his tummy, "is fine dining."

Oliver was still so frightened, that he barely ate a crumb.

"Tonight the chef is preparing roast duckling with herbed potatoes in a delicate cream sauce." Alistair's mouth watered. His whiskers twitched. "One taste and you'll never go back to the country."

The mice crept out of the pantry. The kitchen was empty. They scurried under the chef's work table.

"Our chef is quite a messy fellow," said Alistair. "He drops chunks of meat and potatoes and dollops of sauce all over the floor. One evening I found an entire turkey drumstick lying under the stove."

Alistair darted about, gathering up bits of duckling and potatoes. He didn't notice the chef marching back into the kitchen.

But the chef noticed Alistair.

"You again!" shouted the chef. "And this time you've brought a friend. Furry little pests! I will not have you in my five-star kitchen." The chef grabbed a broom and chased the mice round and round the kitchen.

Alistair and Oliver escaped through a hole under the sink.

"No main course tonight, I'm afraid," said Alistair. "But don't worry, cousin. We'll make up for it with dessert."

Alistair led Oliver around the water pipes and through the walls. They squeezed through a gap in the baseboard, and Oliver found himself in the dining room, directly beneath the pastry cart.

Alistair showed Oliver the tarts and turnovers and cheesecakes. He demonstrated how to flick bits of meringue off a pie with his tail.

Oliver timidly nibbled the edge of a flaky cream puff. It was the most delicious thing he had ever tasted. He leaned forward to get a bigger bite and splat!

The cart lurched forward. Oliver landed face down in the cream puff. Alistair grabbed the edge of a lacy napkin and hung on tight as a waiter wheeled the cart across the dining room.

The cart clanked to a stop near Alistair's apartment. The waiter snatched up three plates of cherry cheesecake and bustled away.

Oliver wobbled off the cart and sank down in the plush carpet to catch his breath. "I'm not cut out for life in the city," he said. "You take too many risks for your dinner. A mouse could starve to death here, too. There is plenty of delicious food, but I'm too frightened to eat any of it. I'm going home to the good life."

So Oliver dragged his carpet bag back through crowded city streets, into subway tunnels, and over fields and valleys until he reached his hole under the root of the big old oak tree.

He ate a late supper of acorns and wheat kernels, then curled up in his oak leaf bed. He could hear the crickets chirping, and he could see fireflies flickering.

Back at his hotel, Alistair licked meringue from his whiskers and curled up in his linen napkin. He listened to the orchestra and watched all the glistening gowns as couples twirled by on the dance floor.

Both mice sighed at the very same time. "I love being home," they said.

Demeter and Persephone

Adapted by Megan Musgrave
Illustrated by Mike Jaroszko

Hades, the king of the Underworld, sat on his lonely throne one day and wished that something could make his world a nicer place to live. The Underworld was cold and dark and dreary, and the sun never shined there. No one ever came to visit Hades because the gates of the Underworld were guarded by Cerberus, a huge, three-headed dog. Cerberus looked so fierce that he scared everyone away.

It made Hades very grumpy to be the king of such a cold and lonely world. "I need a companion who will bring joy to this dark place," said Hades. He decided to disguise himself as a poor traveler and go up to the earth's surface. He would find someone who could help him make the Underworld a happier place to live.

Upon the earth lived Demeter, the goddess of the harvest. Demeter had a beautiful daughter named Persephone. Persephone had long, golden hair and rosy cheeks, and happiness followed her wherever she went. Demeter loved her daughter very much, and she was always full of joy when Persephone was near.

When the goddess of the harvest was happy, the whole world bloomed with life. The fields and orchards were always full of crops to be harvested.

Persephone loved to run through the fields and help Demeter gather food for the people of the earth. But best of all, Persephone loved to play in the apple orchards. There, she could climb the apple trees and pick large, juicy apples to eat.

One day when Hades was visiting the earth, he saw Persephone playing in an apple orchard. He had never seen such a beautiful girl. He stood at the edge of the orchard and watched her while she swung on the branches of the trees.

Finally, Persephone saw Hades standing nearby. In his tattered cloak, he looked like a poor and hungry traveler. Persephone was always generous, so she picked several large apples from the tree and climbed down to meet him. "Please," said Persephone, "take these apples. They will keep you from being hungry on your journey."

Hades thanked Persephone for the apples and went on his way. "I must bring her to the Underworld!" he thought to himself. "It could never be a gloomy place with such a kind and beautiful queen as this!" Then Hades returned to the Underworld.

The next morning, Persephone decided to pick some apples for her mother. She ran to her favorite orchard and began picking the ripest apples she could find.

Suddenly there was a great rumble, and the ground split open before her! Out from below the earth charged two fierce, black horses pulling a dark chariot behind them. On the chariot rode Hades, wearing the black armor of the Underworld.

Persephone tried to run away, but Hades was too quick for her. He caught her and took her away with him in his chariot to the Underworld. The ground closed back up behind them. Not a trace of Persephone was to be seen except a few of the apples she left behind.

When Demeter came home from the fields, Persephone was nowhere to be seen. Demeter went to the orchard where Persephone had been picking apples, and found some apples spilled on the ground. "Something terrible has happened to Persephone!" cried Demeter. She ran to search for her beautiful daughter.

After looking everywhere for her daughter, Demeter decided to visit Helios, the god of the sun. "Helios sees everything that happens on earth. He will help me find Persephone," she said. She went to the great castle of the sun, where Helios was preparing for the end of the day.

"I have seen Persephone," Helios said sadly. He told Demeter that Hades had taken Persephone to the Underworld to be his queen.

"The Underworld!" exclaimed Demeter. She knew how unhappy Persephone would be there. Demeter became very sad and lonely for her daughter. The earth became cold and snowy, and the crops in the field faded and died.

In the Underworld, Persephone was sad and lonely, too. She tried to make her new home a more beautiful place, but nothing helped. The ground was too cold to plant seeds, and there was no sunshine to help them grow. Finally she asked Hades to let her return to the earth.

"But you are the queen of the Underworld!" exclaimed Hades. "Not many girls have the chance to be a queen. I am sure you will be happy here if you only stay a while longer."

Persephone eventually became friends with Cerberus. Although he looked ferocious, he was lonely just like her. Sometimes he walked with her through the gloomy caves of the Underworld.

But even with her new friend, Persephone missed the sunny days and lush fields where she had played on the earth.

Demeter missed her daughter more and more with each passing day. Finally she traveled to Mount Olympus, the home of the gods. She asked Zeus, the most powerful god of all, for his help.

"Hades has kidnapped my daughter Persephone and taken her to the Underworld to be his queen! Please help me bring her back to earth again!" begged Demeter.

Zeus saw that the earth had become cold and barren. He knew that he had to help Demeter so that the earth could become fruitful again. "I will ask Hades to return Persephone," said Zeus sternly. "But if she has eaten any food in the Underworld, I may not be able to help her. Anyone who eats the food of the dead belongs forever to Hades." With that, Zeus took his lightning bolt in hand and traveled to the Underworld.

"Hades!" thundered Zeus when he reached the gates of the Underworld. He made his way inside easily, for even fierce Cerberus was afraid of the king of the gods.

Zeus found Hades sitting sadly on his dark throne, watching Persephone. Persephone hardly looked like the beautiful girl she had been before. Her golden hair had grown dull, and her rosy cheeks were pale.

"Hades, I demand that you return Persephone to the earth. Demeter misses her terribly, and the earth has grown fruitless and barren since you stole her daughter away," said Zeus.

"Very well," sighed Hades. "I thought her beauty would make my Underworld a happier place, but she is only sad and silent since she has come. You may take her back to the earth."

But Hades was very clever. He did not want to lose his queen, so he decided to trick Zeus. When Zeus was getting ready to take Persephone back to earth, Hades took her aside for a moment. He told her she would need food for her journey. He offered her a pomegranate, a large fruit which has juicy seeds to eat. Persephone ate just six pomegranate seeds before she returned to earth. But the pomegranate came from the Underworld. Persephone did not know that Hades had tricked her into eating the food of the dead.

Persephone said good-bye to Cerberus, and Zeus carried her back to the earth and her mother. When Persephone returned, Demeter was overjoyed. She was so happy to be reunited with her daughter that the earth bloomed again, and the crops came back to life. Demeter and Persephone planned to return to their happy life, harvesting good food for the people of the world. But their troubles weren't over yet.

Suddenly, Hades appeared before Demeter and Persephone. "Wait!" he exclaimed. "Persephone has eaten the food of the dead! She ate six seeds from a pomegranate before she came back to earth. She must live in the Underworld forever!"

Demeter and Persephone were upset that Hades had tricked them. Demeter did not want to give up her daughter again. One more time, she asked Zeus for his help.

Zeus was angry about the trick Hades had played, too. He thought very carefully before he decided that Persephone would not have to return to Hades forever.

"But," he said, "you did eat six pomegranate seeds. For each seed that you ate, you will spend one month of the year in the Underworld. The other six months you will spend here on earth with Demeter."

And so each year when Persephone returns to the Underworld, Demeter becomes very sad and lonely for her daughter. Winter comes to the earth, and it is cold and barren. But when Persephone returns to play in the fields with her mother, Demeter is overjoyed. The earth is fruitful and green, and summer reigns until Persephone returns to Hades again.

Paul Revere's Ride

Written by Henry Wadsworth Longfellow
Illustrated by Jon Goodell

Listen, my children, and you shall hear

Of the midnight ride of Paul Revere,

On the eighteenth of April, in Seventy-five,

Hardly a man is now alive

Who remembers that famous day and year.

He said to his friend, "If the British march

By land or sea from the town tonight,

Hang a lantern aloft in the belfry arch

Of the North Church tower as a signal light,

One, if by land, or two, if by sea;

And I on the opposite shore will be,

Ready to ride and spread the alarm

Through every Middlesex village and farm,

For the countryfolk to be up and to arm."

Then he said, "Good night!" and with muffled oar

Silently rowed to the Charlestown shore,

Just as the moon rose over the bay,

Where swinging wide at her moorings lay

The *Somerset*, British man-of-war;

A phantom ship, with each mast and spar

Across the moon like a prison bar,

And a huge black hulk, that was magnified

By its own reflection in the tide.

Meanwhile, his friend, through alley and street,

Wanders and watches with eager ears,

Till in silence around him he hears

The muster of men at the barrack door,

The sound of arms, and the tramp of feet,

And the measured tread of the grenadiers,

Marching down to their boats on the shore.

Then he climbed to the tower of the church,

Up the wooden stairs, with stealthy tread,

To the belfry-chamber overhead,

And startled the pigeons from their perch

On the sombre rafters, that round him made

Masses and moving shapes of shade—

Up the trembling ladder, steep and tall,

To the highest window in the wall,

Where he paused to listen and look down

A moment on the roofs of the town,

And the moonlight flowing over all.

Beneath, in the churchyard, lay the dead,

In their night-encampment on the hill,

Wrapped in silence so deep and still

That he could hear, like a sentinel's tread,

The watchful night-wind, as it went

Creeping along from tent to tent,

And seeming to whisper, "All is well!"

A moment only he feels the spell

On the rising tide, like a bridge of boats.

Of the place and the hour, and the secret dread

Of the lonely belfry and the dead;

For suddenly all his thoughts are bent

On a shadowy something far away,

Where the river widens to meet the bay,

A line of black that bends and floats

On the rising tide, like a bridge of boats.

Meanwhile, impatient to mount and ride,

Booted and spurred, with a heavy stride

On the opposite shore walked Paul Revere.

Now he patted his horse's side,

Now gazed at the landscape far and near,

Then, impetuous, stamped the earth,

And turned and tightened his saddle girth;

But mostly he watched with eager search

The belfry-tower of the Old North Church,

As it rose above the graves on the hill,

Lonely and spectral and sombre and still,

And lo! as he looks, on the belfry's height

A glimmer, and then a gleam of light!

He springs to the saddle, the bridle he turns,

But he lingers and gazes, till full on his sight

A second lamp in the belfry burns!

A hurry of hoofs in a village street,

A shape in the moonlight, a bulk in the dark,

And beneath, from the pebbles, in passing, a spark

Struck out by a steed flying fearless and fleet;

That was all! And yet, through the gloom and the light,

The fate of a nation was riding that night;

And the spark struck out by that steed, in his flight,

Kindled the land into flame with its heat.

He has left the village and mounted the steep,

And beneath him, tranquil and broad and deep,

Is the Mystic, meeting the ocean tides;

And under the alders, that skirt its edge,

Now soft on the sand, now loud on the ledge,

Is heard the tramp of his steed as he rides.

It was twelve by the village clock,

When he crossed the bridge into Medford town.

He heard the crowing of the cock,

And the barking of the farmer's dog,

And felt the damp of the river fog,

That rises after the sun goes down.

It was one by the village clock,

When he galloped into Lexington.

He saw the gilded weathercock

Swim in the moonlight as he passed,

And the meetinghouse windows, blank and bare,

Gaze at him with a spectral glare,

As if they already stood aghast

At the bloody work they would look upon.

It was two by the village clock,

When he came to the bridge in Concord town.

He heard the bleating of the flock,

And the twitter of birds among the trees,

And felt the breath of the morning breeze

Blowing over the meadows brown.

And one was safe and asleep in his bed

Who at the bridge would be first to fall,

Who that day would be lying dead,

Pierced by a British musket ball.

You know the rest. In the books you have read,

How the British Regulars fired and fled,

How the farmers gave them ball for ball,

From behind each fence and farmyard wall,

Chasing the redcoats down the lane,

Then crossing the fields to emerge again

Under the trees at the turn of the road,

And only pausing to fire and load.

So through the night rode Paul Revere;

And so through the night went his cry of alarm

To every Middlesex village and farm,

A cry of defiance and not of fear,

A voice in the darkness, a knock at the door,

And a word that shall echo forevermore!

For, borne on the night-wind of the Past,

Through all our history, to the last,

In the hour of darkness and peril and need,

The people will waken and listen to hear

The hurrying hoofbeats of that steed,

And the midnight message of Paul Revere.

George and the Dragon

Adapted by Brian Conway
Illustrated by Tammie Speer Lyon

T his is the famous tale of St. George and the Dragon. It has been told and told again since his grand adventures over 15 centuries ago, during a time called the Dark Ages, when kings ruled the land, wizards cast spells, and monsters roamed free.

Before St. George became the patron saint of old England, he was just George, a boy who liked to pretend he was a great and brave knight. George lived among the fairies for much of his youth. The queen of fairies had taken him in as a baby, and the fairies raised him as their own. They taught him to be brave and strong, calm and courteous, quick and clever. They taught him to be a noble knight.

At last the time came when George was old enough to seek out his destiny. The queen of fairies called him to see her.

"Your journey starts today," she told him. "You have many adventures before you now. All told, your fantastic quest will take six years. The world is filled with monsters to be slain and battles to be fought. You'll meet kings and paupers, wizards and witches, evil princes and kind princesses."

"Yes, Your Majesty," George bowed before the queen. He was very fond of her. He was sad to leave the land of the Fairies, but he was not afraid.

"Always remember one thing," the queen added, tapping George's silver battle helmet. "Your greatest weapon, George, is your brain."

George traveled many weeks, through many wonderful kingdoms.

"I am a brave and noble knight," he told anyone who asked.

They all said they'd like to hear about his adventures. Sadly, he had none to tell as yet, so he asked them to show him the way of greatest peril. Everyone without hesitation pointed toward the kingdom of Silene. They uttered not a single word more.

As George approached Silene, he noticed the land changed from lush and green to desolate and dark. It seemed the ground had been crossed by fire. There was no grass, only the darkest mud. The trees were bare and black, and a foul stench filled the air.

George walked through this stark land for most of a full day. He did not see a soul—not a bird, not a squirrel, and certainly not a single person.

George finally came to a clearing in the trees. As he looked in the distance, he saw a great castle. A high, solid wall enclosed the castle and the small city around it. The gate was closed up tight. Again, George saw no one around. He moved closer to the gate and saw a young lady creeping quietly through the gate toward him.

"Excuse me, dear lady," he called after her.

"Quiet!" she hushed him. "Have you no sense? You would do well to leave here now and never return."

"But I am a brave knight here to help you," George whispered.

"Alas, sir," the woman replied, "you are but one man. Certainly, you cannot help us."

George looked her in the eyes. "It is my destiny," he told the woman. "I will not go until I have done all I can, even if it costs me my life."

The woman thanked George, then said, "Very well. I am Princess Sabra. Come with me."

They tiptoed through what was once a deep, green forest. Not one bird could be heard singing. As they walked, Sabra explained to George why the kingdom lived in such fear and why the land had been laid to waste.

A fearful dragon had lived in the kingdom for many years, she told him. The horrible beast had ravaged the land, eating helpless animals and destroying almost every living thing in his path. Many men had tried to slay the dragon, but his enormous size, his sharp claws, his vast flapping wings, and his hot breath of fire made the dragon impossible to reach, let alone kill.

At the request of their king, the people had moved with their remaining belongings to protection within the castle walls. By and by, the dragon had run out of animals to eat. Then the dragon demanded food from the people in the kingdom.

"If you do not give me two of your sheep each day," the Dragon roared, "I will come through those walls for my breakfast!"

The princess told George that her father had no choice. He ordered his subjects to give up two of their sheep every day for several weeks. Each morning as the sun rose, so rose the dragon from his lair between the mountains on the other side of the lake. He ate the sheep and left the people of the kingdom alone.

"The dragon sleeps now," said the princess, "but we gave up our last two sheep this very morning. Tomorrow we shall have nothing to give the dragon, and we shall all perish."

"Then I have arrived at the right time," said George bravely. "I will slay this dragon immediately."

"No," said Sabra harshly. "You would never survive alone."

They came to a cave in the dark forest. "To slay the dragon," Sabra told George, "we need help. That is why we are here." She pointed to the opening of the cave and began to enter.

In the cave there lived a wise old hermit. Only the king's royal family, and now George, knew about this hermit. Some said he was a sorcerer over 900 years old, but no one knew for sure. He advised the royal family in times of great despair. Never was the hermit's wisdom needed more than at this moment.

Sabra and George crept up to the hermit, who stared into his fire. He did not turn to look at them, but he spoke as if he knew they were coming. The hermit's voice rumbled through the cave.

> Long ago it was told,
>
> Two brave knights would come to know,
>
> The only way to save the rest:
>
> The Serpent's weakness in his breath.

With those words an ancient hourglass appeared at their feet. George bent down to pick it up.

George did not understand. He asked the strange little man, but the hermit would speak no more.

When George and Sabra left the cave, it was already dark. They knew they must hurry to the dragon's lair. If they had any hope of destroying the fierce creature, they had to get there while the dragon slept.

"The hermit speaks in puzzles," Sabra sighed. "What do we do with this ancient timepiece?"

George remembered what the queen of fairies had told him. His best weapon, she had said, was his brain. He studied the hourglass closely. The tiny blue grains of sand fell through to the bottom of the glass one by one. Each bit of sand looked like a magic crystal frozen in time.

They arrived at the lake. George and Sabra walked softly through the fog so they would not be heard. The sands in the hourglass dropped with every careful step.

George thought he might like to have his sword at this moment, but he felt he must have faith in what the Queen had said. He truly did not know what would happen at the dragon's lair.

"The time left in the hourglass will lead us," George whispered. "We must wait until all the sand has dropped through, then we should know what to do."

"We should know?" Sabra asked. "And what shall happen if we don't?"

Sadly, George had no answer for her. He mumbled, "We shall wait."

The smell as they approached the lair was horrible. No one had ever been so close to the dragon before, and not a soul had ever been brave enough, or perhaps foolish enough, to dare enter the dragon's lair.

George and the princess set George's shield near the sleeping dragon's head. There they were protected from the dragon's snores, when hot blasts of fire poured from his scaly nose. They watched the icy blue sands tick away, and they waited.

Suddenly the dragon stirred. The sun was coming up behind the mountains. Now Sabra thought they would not have a chance to see the sand run through the hourglass. Surely the dragon would find them first. The dragon raised himself up and rubbed his slimy eyes.

As George watched the dragon rise, he stopped watching the hourglass! The very last grain of sand was dropping through. At that very moment, the dragon stretched and yawned a great, fiery yawn.

"Now, George!" Sabra shouted.

George knew what must be done. He threw the hourglass up, up, up to the dragon's yawning mouth. It shattered on the dragon's slithering tongue in a cloud of icy mist.

Now our two heroes had sorely angered the dragon. He looked down to see them. Both George and Sabra ducked behind the shield. The dragon reared back to hurl a fiery blast at them. But, as fortune would have it, only cool ice and soft snow came from the dragon's mouth. The dragon took a deep breath, certain the furnace inside of him would melt the ice.

But, the hermit's magic had changed the dragon. His mouth shut tight with frozen ice, the once-fearsome dragon jumped into the deep, warm lake. Only there could he keep from freezing from the inside out.

That dragon never bothered another soul. Some see him coming up for air on occasion, but only on very warm nights. The dragon would not dare stay out of the warm water too long, for fear of becoming a giant icy statue.

George and Sabra had saved the kingdom. They arrived at the castle to hear great cries of joy and triumph.

The king offered George all he had in thanks, but George wanted no payment for his deeds.

"I have many more adventures left to face," George told the people. "They are my greatest reward."

George shared the story of the dragon of Silene along his journey. And it is still told today. That is how George, the brave knight from the land of the fairies, earned his sainthood.

The Boy Who Cried Wolf

Adapted by Mary Rowitz
Illustrated by Jon Goodell

There was a young boy who lived in a village. He wasn't very old, but he had an important job to do. He was a shepherd, and his job was to guard the sheep from danger, especially the wolves who lived in the forest.

The shepherd boy also had to make sure the sheep got plenty of food and exercise. Every day, in order to give the sheep the exercise they needed, the boy took them to a nearby valley. Once they had walked there, the sheep would graze on the tasty green grass that grew in the valley. The villagers trusted the shepherd to take good care of the sheep.

The shepherd boy wasn't really all alone. The village people worked nearby. If a wolf ever did attack, the people could run to the rescue.

The villagers counted on the shepherd boy to do his job. They never felt that they had to check on him. They trusted him to do his best.

Every day, the shepherd faithfully watched the sheep from his lookout post. He could also see the people hard at work. Some days they worked at their jobs in the village. Sometimes they did other chores.

For the shepherd boy, every day was the same. He looked at the sheep. They looked the same every day. Then he looked out at the forest. It looked the same, too. While he was happy most days just to do his job, some days he wished that something exciting would happen.

In his whole life, the boy had never seen a wolf come near the sheep. In fact, he had never even seen a wolf! Some people told stories of hearing wolves howl in the forest, but the boy never heard any howling.

One day the shepherd thought, "Maybe I can play some games with the sheep. That would be exciting." He planned his next day, and he smiled when he thought about the fun he would have.

The boy woke up bright and early the next morning. He ate his breakfast very quickly and then packed his bag for the day. He kissed his parents good-bye and hurried to take the sheep to the valley.

As soon as they reached the green grass in the valley, the shepherd boy tried to play games with the sheep. The sheep, however, had a different idea.

All the sheep wanted to do was eat grass or take a nap. "This isn't any fun at all," thought the shepherd boy. Feeling downhearted, he walked back to his lookout post.

Then something caught the corner of his eye. "I wonder," he said, "what is on the other side of those trees?" The boy smiled to himself. Would it be so bad to pretend there was a wolf? He thought this would be a good joke.

As the sheep ate the grass, he cupped his hand near his mouth and shouted, "Wolf! Wolf! A wolf is stealing the sheep! Come help me!"

All the village people stopped what they were doing and ran to help scare off the wolf. When they got there, they were very confused.

The villagers did not find a wolf. And where was the shepherd? They were worried about him. What if the wolf had stolen the boy? Frantically, they began to search high and low to find him.

A villager pointed to a tree and said, "There he is over there. Is he okay?" They saw he was not hurt. In fact, he was laughing!

"You looked so funny running up here for no reason. This was a great joke," laughed the boy.

The villagers did not laugh. They shook their heads and said, "We have to get back to work now. We don't have time for pranks."

The shepherd boy didn't hear a word they said. He was laughing too hard.

At breakfast the next day, the boy's mother and father told him to be good. He nodded his head and left to tend the sheep. Soon, however, he was bored again. "Wolf! Wolf!" he shouted, louder than the day before. "A wolf is stealing the sheep! Come help me!"

Again the villagers came running. Again there was no wolf in sight. This time the villagers were very upset. They told the boy, "If you don't tell people the truth all the time, they will never know when to believe you."

The boy was still laughing at his joke. After the villagers went back to their jobs, however, he started to think about what the people had said. "Maybe," he thought, "it isn't so funny to play tricks on others." The boy began walking back to his lookout post. Little did he know he was soon going to have all the excitement he could handle.

Just on the other side of the trees, a sly wolf had seen everything. When the shepherd boy reached his post, the wolf began stealing the sheep. The shepherd boy couldn't believe his eyes. It was a real wolf! He cried out, "Wolf! Wolf! A wolf is stealing the sheep! Come help me!"

He waited for the villagers to come running, but no one came. They weren't going to fall for that trick again! This time, though, it was no trick.

The boy tried yelling for help again, but no one came. He could only watch as the wolf ran off into the forest with all the sheep.

The shepherd boy ran into the village. "Wolf! Wolf!" he cried. "He's stealing our sheep!" The boy kept running and calling for help, but no one believed he was telling the truth. He called out again, "Wolf! Wolf!"

"I bet!" said one villager. "I can't believe that boy is trying to make fools out of us again."

"Well, he's not going to make a fool out of me," said another villager. "I don't believe him."

Finally the shepherd boy stopped running. "I'm telling the truth this time," he said. "There really is a wolf in the valley, and he really is stealing the sheep. You've got to believe me."

The villagers came and looked at the boy. They shook their fingers at him. "We're smarter than you think," the people said. "This time we're just going to ignore you and your wolf! Humph!"

At that moment, the shepherd boy knew no one would believe him. How could he blame them? When they trusted him, he let them down. He lost their trust by not always telling the truth.

He sadly walked back to his lookout post and gazed down where he always took his sheep to eat grass. But there weren't any sheep left. The wolf had taken all of them away. The boy was so sad that he began to cry.

The shepherd boy didn't think his joke was funny anymore.

The Little Dutch Boy

Adapted by Sarah Toast
Illustrated by Linda Dockey Graves

Long ago there was a boy named Hans who lived with his mother in a pretty town in Holland. The land of Holland is very flat, and much of it is below the level of the sea. The farmers there built big walls called dikes to keep the sea from flooding their farms. Hans and the other children knew that if a dike broke, the fields and towns would be ruined.

One day Hans's mother packed a basket of fruit, bread, and cheese for Hans to take to their old friend, Mr. Van Notten. Mr. Van Notten lived outside of town, and it was a long way to his house. As Hans set out on his walk, his mother told him not to stay too late. She wanted him to be home before it got dark.

Mr. Van Notten had only an old dog to keep him company, so he was very happy when Hans came to visit him. To get to Mr. Van Notten's home, Hans just followed the main road out of town. The road ran right alongside the dike.

Hans was very thirsty and hungry after his long walk, so Mr. Van Notten made hot cocoa and set out the bread and cheese. After their meal, the boy and the old man talked by the fire. Hans enjoyed Mr. Van Notten's stories of the olden days.

When Mr. Van Notten's dog scratched at the door to be let out, Hans noticed that the sky had become dark and stormy. He decided that he should leave right away to get home before it started to rain. "Good-bye," Hans said, "I'll come back to visit you soon, Mr. Van Notten."

"Good-bye, dear boy," said Mr. Van Notten. "Be careful."

Hans walked quickly, but he was not even halfway home when the air became much colder and the wind began to blow very hard. It wasn't long before cold, stinging raindrops battered Hans as he struggled against the powerful wind. The weather made it difficult for Hans to walk, but he kept going. "If I just keep putting one foot in front of the other," said Hans to himself, "I'll be home soon." He repeated this to himself as he walked against the wind.

The strong wind made the trees bend low, and it flattened the pretty flowers. Hans was getting cold, and he had to hold his hat on his head to keep it from blowing away. "I hope my mother isn't upset when I arrive home so cold and wet," he thought.

Hans was getting more and more tired with every step, but he had to keep going. He remembered that his mother wanted him home before dark, and Hans did not want to let her down. He wanted to get home so she would not worry.

Hans kept his head down against the wind as he trudged along the road. It was so dark outside that Hans had no idea he was nearing the town until he lifted his head for a moment. Hans was happy to see the dike right in front of him. It meant he would soon be home and out of the rain.

Even with all the raindrops falling and dripping from the trees, Hans noticed some water where it shouldn't have been. There was a small hole in the dike, and a trickle of water was seeping through.

Hans knew right away what must have happened. The storm had whipped up the waves of the sea on the other side, and the great weight of the pounding water made a crack in the dike.

"I've got to warn everybody that the dike has sprung a leak!" thought Hans to himself.

Hans ran into town. "The dike is breaking!" he shouted. "Help! We've got to fix the dike!"

Shout as he would, no one heard Hans. Nobody else was outside, and all the houses had been completely shut because of the storm. All the doors were secured tightly and bolted, every window closed and shuttered. Every streetlamp had been blown out.

Hans soon realized his shouting wasn't doing any good. He stopped running to catch his breath. Leaning against a fence, Hans tried to think of what he should do next.

Hans knew his mother must be worrying about him, but he also knew that the tiny hole in the dike was getting bigger every minute. If the hole got big enough, the sea would surely push its way through and break the dike. If the dike broke, all would be lost. The sea would flood the farms and wash away the pretty little town.

As fast as he could, Hans ran back to the place where he had seen the water seeping through the dike. Sure enough, the crack was bigger now than when he first had spotted it. Hans knew that the crack must be fixed soon. Otherwise the sea would break through, and it would be too late. There was nothing else to do, so Hans balled up his fist and pushed it into the hole to stop the little stream of water.

Hans was proud and happy that one small boy could hold back the sea. He was sure that his worried mother would soon send people to look for him. But minutes turned into hours as Hans patiently stood there.

As darkness fell Hans became very cold and tired, and his arm began to ache. He had to force himself to keep standing on his tired legs.

As Hans stood in the cold rain by the dike, he thought about the warmth of the fireplace at home. Then he thought about how good it would feel to lie down in his bed. These thoughts helped the exhausted boy get through the long night.

When Hans didn't come home that evening, his mother began to worry. Even while the rain was falling, she kept looking out the door for Hans to return. At last she decided that Hans must have waited out the storm at Mr. Van Notten's. She thought he must have spent the night there because it was too dark to come home after the storm.

After looking out the door one more time, Hans's mother closed up the house and went to bed, but she couldn't sleep. She was too worried about her little boy.

Early the next morning, Mr. Van Notten was walking to Hans's home. He wanted to thank Hans for the visit and thank his mother for the tasty food. When he came to where Hans was, the boy was trembling with cold.

Hans's arm hurt from the effort of keeping his fist in the hole of the dike, and his legs were ready to collapse from standing all night. Still Hans had to hold firm for just a little while longer. Mr. Van Notten ran into town to get help.

"Don't worry, Hans," said Mr. Van Notten. "I'll be back in a jiffy. You're doing a great job, just hang on a little longer." Soon Mr. Van Notten returned with someone to take care of Hans and materials to repair the dike.

Hans was wrapped in blankets and carried home. He was put to bed and given warm broth to drink. His mother rubbed his fingers and his stiff legs.

Word quickly spread through the town of how Hans had held back the sea all by himself. The townspeople were very curious. They went to the dike to see the hole that Hans had bravely kept plugged.

As soon as Hans felt strong enough, he and his mother went back to the dike to see the repairs that were being made. Everyone in town was overjoyed to see Hans. They thanked him for holding back the mighty sea and for saving them from what would have otherwise been a terrible flood.

The mayor of the town presented Hans with a medal to honor his dedication, and all the townspeople cheered loudly. Hans would forever after be remembered as a hero. Years later, even after Hans was all grown up, people still called him the little boy with the big heart.

The Four Musicians

Adapted by Mary Rowitz
Illustrated by Wendy Edelson

One day a donkey was walking along the fence by the barn, singing softly to himself. He stopped when he heard his owner talking with another farmer. The donkey leaned in closer so he could hear what the two were discussing. "I know what you mean," the one farmer said. "Sometimes it's easier to just get a younger one."

The donkey wondered what they could be talking about. His owner continued, "I just can't find many reasons to keep the tired bag of bones around much longer. He is very old and cannot pull the plow anymore. It's time to put that old donkey out to pasture."

The donkey couldn't believe his ears! They were talking about him! He was very hurt to hear these words.

"Hee-haw!" said the donkey. "I won't be sent out to pasture. I'll go to the town of Bremen and become a musician."

The donkey had just started on his way when he saw a sad dog sitting by the road. The donkey asked what was bothering him. "My owner says I am too old to hunt," howled the dog. "He wants to get a dog who keeps quiet."

"I have a thought that may interest you. Why don't you come to Bremen, and we will work as musicians," said the donkey. "We'll be quite a team."

"Woof!" said the dog. "I like that idea!" The two new pals had not gone far before they crossed paths with a gloomy cat. They asked what was wrong.

"My owner says I am too old to catch mice," he cried.

They invited the cat to come to Bremen to sing with them. "Mee-ow!" answered the cat, and the three were on their way.

The dog, cat, and donkey were walking along when a very upset rooster flew into the middle of the road. "Cock-a-doodle-day!" the rooster squawked.

"What a strong voice you have!" the dog said.

"My owners say there is no point in having a strong voice if you don't use it every day," crowed the rooster. "I cannot get up early enough to wake up the workers anymore. My owners plan to serve me for Sunday dinner!"

"Join us on our trip," said the dog. "We're going to work as musicians. We could really use your strong voice to make our band complete."

"Cock-a-doodle-day!" said the rooster. "Let's be on our way!" The four new friends practiced singing as they walked toward Bremen.

Nighttime came. Just when the four musicians found a nice tree to camp under, the rooster began to squawk. "I think I see a light shining from inside a house!" he said. "It doesn't seem far away."

"They might have some food to share," said the dog. "A big, juicy bone sounds mighty good right about now."

"I think a big bowl of milk would be absolutely purr-fect," purred the cat.

The four musicians walked up to the house. The donkey, being the tallest of the group, peered inside the window. "What do you see?" the cat asked as he tried to get a glimpse.

"Well, there are four men sitting at a table that is covered with food," the donkey said. "There are stacks of gold everywhere."

"What do we do now?" asked the rooster.

"Remember, we are going to be musicians," the donkey said. "We should practice singing for our supper."

The four musicians decided to stand one on top of the other so everyone could be heard. First the donkey took his place near the bottom of the window. Then the dog jumped on his back. The cat made his way up to the dog's back. Finally the rooster flew to the top.

Even though the four friends had practiced their singing all day, they were still a little bit nervous. They turned to face the window and cleared their throats. The donkey gave the signal, and they began to sing.

Never has there been a louder or mightier group effort! The four friends tried to sing better than they ever had before. What they didn't know is that it didn't sound like singing. It sounded like, "Hee-haw! Woof! Mee-ow! Cock-a-doodle-day!"

The four friends also didn't know that the men inside were robbers. When the robbers heard the loud noise, they looked out the window. They saw what looked like a four-headed beast. "Run! Run! Run!" one robber yelled. "Run before the four-headed beast gets us!"

The animals were confused. Why had the men run away? The donkey said, "I believe I know what is happening. Our audience enjoyed our singing so much that they are going to get more people to hear our concert."

"I say we go inside, have some dinner as a reward for our splendid singing, and wait for our audience to return," the rooster said.

"Indeed!" agreed the donkey. "That is a grand idea!" The four musicians went into the house.

The four musicians were so hungry they ate everything! It didn't take long to decide that the life of a musician would suit them very well indeed.

Soon after the meal, they were very sleepy. Since they were already inside the house, they agreed it would be best to spend the night there. After all, they didn't want to miss the people who were coming to hear them perform.

There was plenty of room for everyone in the house. The donkey lay in the middle of the room. The dog stretched out by the door. The cat curled up near the fireplace, and the rooster flew to a ceiling beam.

Soon their sleepy heads began nodding. It didn't take long for their tired eyes to close. They were all sound asleep when the doorknob slowly began to turn. They were still asleep when someone tiptoed into the room.

One robber had come back to see if he could get some of the gold. It was quite dark, and he needed some light to find his way around. He thought he saw a glow from the coals in the fireplace. But the glow was coming from the cat's eyes. When he lit a match to start a fire, the cat jumped. The robber tripped over the dog. The dog bit his leg, causing the robber to stumble over the donkey. The donkey kicked the robber. The noise woke the rooster, and he began crowing, "Cock-a-doodle-day! Leave without delay!"

The robber ran as fast as his legs would carry him. He told the others to stay away forever or the four-headed beast would get them.

The four musicians lived in the house for the rest of their days. They were quite happy giving free concerts and using the gold to buy food.

THE
END